Lawrence

The Perfect Christmas

Karen Tucci

True Heart Romance

Contents

Karen's Other Books:

Stand Alone Books:

<u>When the Dust Settles: A Sweet Romance with a Navy SEAL</u>

G & G Security Series (Coming 2025)

(The characters from When the Dust Settles cross-over in this series)

Operation: Heal my SEAL Book 1

Operation: Find my SEAL Book 2

Operation: Keep my SEAL Book 3

Operation: Train my SEAL Book 4

Second Chance Series:

<u>Starting Over</u>

<u>Moving On</u>

Big L' Ranch Series

<u>The Perfect Kiss: Book 1</u>

<u>The Perfect: Cowboy Book 2</u>

<u>The Perfect Match Book 3</u>

<u>The Perfect Christmas (Holiday Novella)</u>

<u>The Perfect Sheriff Book 5</u>

Best Friends Series

<u>Let Me Carry You</u>

<u>Let Me Marry You</u>

YA Cumberland Christian Prep School Series

The Big Score (Coming 2025)

Chapter 1

Christmas was always a hard time of the year for Sean Lawrence. *Smile and nod.* He ordered himself, as many parishioners greeted him. It was the beginning of December and it looked like Christmas had tossed its sugar cookies all over town.

Sean appreciated Pastor Myles's subtlety and elegance for decorating. He displayed a rustic manger in front of the pulpit and the tree in the corner had ornaments that worshippers put on to remember their lost loved ones.

Raddix and Lily, Sean's son and daughter-in-law, respectively, were at the fake evergreen hanging an ornament for Sara, Raddix's mom and Sean's late wife.

Sean met Sara when they were seventeen, married when they were eighteen, and had Raddix before they turned nineteen. She was the love of his life, so when Sara died in a freak storm, Sean withdrew from everyone, except his cattle. For years, he'd wondered why God took Sara away from him that quickly.

Sadly, Raddix had only been five when his mother died in that storm. Sean held onto guilt, the size of Montana, believing he failed Raddix, but he never gave himself credit for being the vessel God used to save his son from that same storm.

A warm hand brushed along his shoulder, jolting him. He knew who it was without looking. Her touch heated him through his signature flannel shirt.

"Good Morning, Sean," Violet's soft voice hit him in the gut.

All at once, Sean rose from his seat, wiping his clammy hands on the front of his dark blue jeans he only wore to church or special gatherings. "G-good morning, Violet," he stammered as she dropped eye contact and moved to her seat with her friends, also known as the town's grandmas or Troublesome Trio.

Stop looking at her now. The gold belt wrapped around her small waist, cinching the two-toned red dress she teased Sean with this morning exposed her curves. Every. Single. One. He only saw her dressed up on Sundays. Other times she was expressing her creativity at her flower shop in jeans and a t-shirt or sweatshirt. It didn't matter what this woman wore, it clung right to where it should. Sean ripped his eyes from Violet as he sank back into his seat. *What would Sara think? Please forgive me.*

Again, he made the mistake of looking in Violet's direction. Instead of connecting with her, the troublemakers Hazel, Myrtle, and Doris waved at him and smiled knowingly. Sean nodded with ease, but his insides were screaming, *Don't let me be their next victim!*

"Dad," Raddix pulled Sean's attention from the front of the sanctuary with a smile of his own. It was almost like Raddix forgot what he wanted to say as shared a look with his wife.

"That was a gorgeous ornament you chose, Sean," Lily stated as they sat in the pew. "Sara's hand-written name along the top was perfect."

"Thanks."

The closer it got to Christmas, the more Sean struggled. This year, however, it seemed different. He couldn't escape the deep sorrow that had haunted him since he lost Sara, but an intense pang of something else accompanied it, waging a war within Sean that he wasn't able to fight until he comprehended what he was dealing with.

As if they had a mind of their own, Sean's eyes drifted back to Violet and his stomach lurched. *Lord, please don't toy with me! I cannot allow myself to have those types of feelings for her.*

"Welcome friends and family," Pastor Myles's voice sang through the speakers as he pressed his glasses higher onto his nose. Every Sunday, he seemed happy to deliver his message.

As the pastor waited for everyone to settle in their seats, Sean quietly continued to observe others. If he was a betting man, based on the lively conversation and soft looks being shared, something between their sheriff and Willow, the pastor's daughter, was imminent.

"Good to see you, Sean. Raddix." Gerard, Haven Ridge's sheriff, shook hands with the men. "Lily," he acknowledged her with a head nod.

"Are you coming over to watch Tanner compete?" Raddix asked Gerard, whose eyes were fixed on Willow walking to her seat.

Tanner befriended everyone at the ranch. Once the Nationals concluded, he would be working at Big L' Ranch full time.

"You can bring a *friend* if you'd like," Raddix chuckled, earning him a little jab in the ribs from his wife.

"Don't tease him. I think they're cute."

"Who? Yeah, no. . . we're not a thing," Gerard stumbled. "I'm on call, but I might be able to stop in for a little while," he answered the initial question and hurried to his seat. Chances are Gerard hoped his flustered appearance would go unnoticed.

Raddix is a troublemaker just like Violet's friends. Compassion for the sheriff sat on Sean's chest. To be honest, Sean would have words with his son if he tried that nonsense with him. No man should have to feel uncomfortable like that. As if on cue, Violet's friends were gawking at him again. *Dear God, please help me.*

"This is not my normal sermon today, but don't worry, I'll bring that next week. Knowing someone needed to hear it, God placed this message on my heart yesterday."

The people in the congregation laughed, including Sean. Pastor Myles was a true man of God, praying and listening to the Creator.

"I know you've all heard the Christmas story beautifully depicted in Luke's gospel. At Christmas time we showcase God coming to earth as an innocent baby; a gift to the world and that idea is where I'm going to focus today."

To his right, Sean noticed Raddix shift, resting his ankle on top of his other thigh and draped his arm around Lily.

Sean glimpsed at Violet, only able to see her profile, and sighed inwardly.

"Paul tells us in Romans chapter five how Adam's sin brought death upon everyone after him and Eve. He's referring to spiritual death." Pastor Myles started pacing on the stage as he delivered his message. "We are all born separated from God, but thanks to an abundance of undeserved grace through Jesus, the gift of salvation is available for all men."

Sean stretched out his legs, crossing his ankles while he skimmed the rest of the chapter as Pastor Myles continued preaching.

Concern filled his chest when Pastor Myles glanced at him, confirming that the sermon was directed toward him.

"Many people out there reject God's gift of salvation. To those who have accepted that gift, don't think you're off the hook. We all have rejected a gift from God at some point, either intentionally or unintentionally."

Sean crossed his arms over his chest, trying to figure out what gift had God ever given him that he rejected.

"As we approach the day we celebrate as Christ's birthday, reflect on every gift God's given you. Yes, he gave us the ability to choose the ultimate gift–eternal life with him–but what else has He given you? It might be a spiritual gift, a monetary one, a living one."

Sean's chest tightened and worry wormed through his veins. The pastor's impromptu sermon was intended for someone here. He believed God worked that way. Was *he* the someone? Had God given him a gift that he ignored?

"Have you accepted it willingly or are you still fighting a gift from the Lord?" Pastor Miles wrapped up his sermon. All the while Sean distracted himself, wondering if there was a connection between the message and him.

Trying to hide his distress when he noticed Violet must have slipped out during his musing, Sean gripped the back of the pew in front of him and pulled himself up to his full height–six feet three inches in his boots.

Sean was never one to stay after church and chit-chat. He quickly scanned the room, finding Raddix with the other men from the ranch, waiting for their wives.

He stopped before the group, asking, "Why are you all huddled here when we could be back at the ranch getting ready for Tanner's first event?"

"It'll record," Damon stated as he rocked on his heels with his arms crossed over his chest.

Damon was a former bronc rider and Tanner's teammate, anxious to watch his friend last the full eight seconds.

"Maybe you guys should carpool home and leave the women your keys to get back," Sean suggested, trying to channel his own angst. "What are they doing, anyway?"

Quinton, the ranch foreman, motioned to the other side of the sanctuary.

Violet stood amongst the men's wives and other women from the congregation. Her full smile slightly crinkled the corner of her eyes, easing some of the tension in Sean's chest.

"Would you leave if you were waiting for one of those beautiful ladies?" Raddix goaded his dad with a wry, slightly amused smile.

He gave the men a sheepish grin. *I'll fix you, Son—think you can out smart your old man.*

"Yup. See ya at the ranch."

Sean paraded to the door, accepting well wishes, handshakes, and hugs from some of the older parishioners.

He stopped at the double doors. No doubt his son was watching him with precision, and he stole a quick glance in Violet's direction. When their eyes met, she rewarded him with a wide smile.

Sean's heart pounded harder than Apple Jack's hooves, and he realized what was coming. The war within him was unavoidable ever since he started becoming close to Violet. Sean let his gut reaction to flee overpowered him yet again.

Turning, he shook the pastor's hand and rushed to the parking lot. It was that moment when the Lord spoke to him and he froze, his hand gripping the truck's door handle.

Could it be Violet?

Chapter 2

"Go get 'em, Tanner," Sean yelled at the television as everyone at the ranch gathered in the living room to watch Tanner at Nationals.

Amelia, Sean's niece and owner of Big L' Ranch, came rushing to her husband's side. "Quinton, is he on?"

"No, it's just the line-up of competitors," Quinton's deep laugh irked Sean.

Damon added his own chortle. "Someone might be a little tense."

Sean's muscles tightened. Damon must be alluding to Sean's discomfort at church when he disappeared.

Amelia returned to the kitchen requesting, "Let me know when Tanner is *actually* competing."

Sean passed behind the former bronc competitor and shoved his shoulder. Damon and Sean were both tall, stocky men, so it didn't surprise him when Damon held his own.

"Watch it Richards," Sean's warning dropped there, not sure what he'd threaten the man with since he had it all—the beautiful wife he saved from her demonic parents; three wonderful children from a previous marriage: Dean, Dominic, and Darlene; and a new one on the way.

Bingo! That was his leverage. "Hey, Damon, do you have anything you'd like to share with the group?" Sean's antagonizing voice rang out.

Yes, Sean had achieved an all-time low with his comment. He'd never betray Damon, and the man knew it. Damon didn't even flinch, giving it right back. "You first, cattleman."

Sean didn't miss the glint in Damon's eye. The younger man was quick-witted. Sean murmured, "I think we're good," as he settled on the loveseat.

"Dad, will you come help me?" Raddix hollered from the kitchen.

When he entered the room, Sean jumped, punching his fist in the air as the singing snowman greeted him with a rendition of Jingle Bells. Laughter erupted from the living room, and it wasn't only the kids. It was nice having them on the ranch, especially at Christmas.

Thanks to the tweens and teens, Christmas was in full swing. Stockings adorned the mantle, while garland encircled the banister leading upstairs. A seven-foot blue fir stood in the corner, garnished with homemade and store-bought decorations. A mistletoe hung nearby, and the kids teased Emmanuel about it. They wondered how long it would take for him to kiss Damon's youngest, Darlene, under the sprig.

Ever since he'd arrived, Emmanuel had been enamored with Darlene. If he was anything like his dad, Quinton, Emmanuel would win the girl one day.

"Whatcha need, Son?" Sean asked, stopping beside Raddix at the counter.

"Will you bring the crackers and cheese to the living room once I put them on the platter?"

Sean nodded. "Sure will."

"Thanks." Raddix handed bowls of chips and dip to Amelia, who escaped to the living room.

"Everything okay in there?" he asked as he cut the cheese into cubes.

"They've interviewed Tanner, but we're still waiting for his event."

"That's not what I was referring to." Raddix chortled out a laugh, but suppressed it, letting his concerned expression overrule.

"I'm not sure what you're talking about, Son," Sean grumbled, knowing what Raddix would say.

"You have feelings for Violet." It wasn't a question. Raddix's boldness made Sean defensive.

No. He's way off. With his arm crossed over his chest, Sean opened his mouth to share his thoughts, refuting his son's statement, but nothing came out.

A car door slammed in the distance, grabbing Sean's attention. Then, a familiar voice sang to him.

"Hello. Is it okay to come in?"

Violet. What is she doing here?

Without thinking, Sean ran his fingers through his hair and tugged the hem of his shirt down. *I wish I had my hat.* He spied Raddix looking at him, forcing his lips to remain neutral.

"What?"

Raddix shrugged, suppressing a grin. "Nothing."

Sean cleared his throat. "We're in here."

Rushing to help ease her full arms, he said, "Let me take something for you."

She brought more chips, crackers, dips, and jam in one bag and a hot broccoli and chicken braid on a round cooking stone in her other hand.

Sean set down the stone for Violet. He clenched his fist, resisting the urge to pull her close and brush the snowflakes from her hair and slender shoulders. He towered over her, and it wasn't the first time he'd wondered how she'd feel in his arms.

"You looked stunning in your dress earlier," Sean blurted out, dumbfounded.

Violet's eyebrows raised, not expecting that compliment. "I guess jeans and t-shirt won't cut it for this get together," her tone light, letting Sean know she was teasing.

"You look fabulous now. You can keep your clothes on." Sean pressed his palms into his eye sockets, hoping when he opened them, Violet wouldn't be standing in front of him. But she was.

"Real smooth, Dad," Raddix teased from behind. "You always told me to wait for marriage. Good thing I'm married, or I'd say you were a bad influence."

"Shut it," Sean spoke low and out of the corner of his mouth, but that only encouraged Raddix to laugh harder.

Because of Violet's sweetness, Sean couldn't tell if she was amused or appalled by his foot-in-mouth fiasco. A queasy feeling assaulted Sean. Before he could stop himself, he tried again.

"I mean, you look great in what you have on. I wouldn't want you to take your clothes off for me."

Raddix slapped the cheese knife on the counter. "That isn't any better. I suggest you stop talking."

"Oh, no. Please continue. I find this very entertaining," Violet chimed.

Her eyes, the color of light amber honey, sparkled when she looked at Sean. His eyes dipped to her lips long enough to ogle the tip of her tongue brushing along her bottom lip, and her teeth tugging said lip inward.

Is it hot in here?

He returned his focus to Violet's eyes, but they were just as dangerous. She had the softest brown eyes he'd ever seen. He often wondered if they were begging him for more.

This had been their mantra for the past year. Neither one willing to make a move, nor express the growing chemistry between the two of them, but her eyes and body language divulged an unspoken desire. For the most part, Sean had accepted being alone, but now, whenever he was around her, a feeling akin to longing ripped at his insides that he continued to brush off. Admittedly, it was getting harder to ignore.

If I kissed her, I'd pull her off the ground to avoid getting a stiff neck. Violet was about a foot shorter than Sean.

What!? Why am I thinking about kissing her? Or anyone, for that matter. What would Sara think?

When she looked up at him again with a soft, lingering gaze, his breath hitched. He didn't mean for that to happen, but it was unavoidable.

"This awkward encounter is too much for me, so I'll bring this to the living room and give you some privacy," Raddix announced before he escaped.

"Here. I brought your flowers, so you didn't have to make a special trip to town tomorrow," she paused.

How thoughtful is this woman? Raddix said it was obvious Violet liked me. Maybe he was right. A man's deceased wife would intimidate most women, especially one he'd described as the angelic love of his life. Not Violet. Nothing seemed to intimidate her.

"If you want to wait until tomorrow, just put them in water, and they'll be fine." she finished.

Sean's heart thumped against his ribcage. He hated how much her kindness got to him. His heart shouldn't be flipping and flopping like a teenager. Nor should his pulse be pounding like a sledgehammer, threatening to burst an artery.

Violet's eyes roamed over him with ease, warming his chest even more.

Her husband died only four years ago. How is she ready to move on? Is she the abnormal one or is it me?

"Thank you. That was very thoughtful of you." Their fingers brushed when Violet handed him the flowers. The little jolts of electricity, which had been happening for quite some time whenever they'd touched, were getting stronger and less coincidental.

Sean took the flowers to Sara's grave at that instant. He needed to figure things out before he made a mistake or hurt Violet's feelings.

Chapter 3

What did I say? Violet thought as Sean ran out with the flowers.

After months of waiting, his sapphire eyes finally warmed up to her, but then he bolted, leaving Violet in the kitchen alone.

His uncharacteristic, nervous rambling made her legs tremble, and her heart soared. Could he be interested in her?

Unless Violet's internal man reader, as Myrtle called it, crashed, which she didn't believe it did, Sean Lawrence's body language screamed *I want you!*

At least, that's what Violet prayed, hoping God didn't mind her petitioning Him for a chance at love.

Love? Slow down, Vi, give the man space. She scoffed at the inner battle between her thoughts and feelings. Violet had watched Sean honor his wife every week with flowers, and she helped him. Meanwhile, Violet's feelings for him had continued to grow, leaving her trapped in a sea of uncertainty.

"Violet," Raddix interrupted her musing. While looking around, he inquired, "Is everything okay?"

"Mm-hmm."

Violet stepped around Raddix with her dip and cheese platter. He opened the refrigerator door.

She whispered, "Thank you."

After shutting it, Raddix leaned his shoulder against the stainless steel appliance, reminding her of Sean.

"Give him time. He'll stop beating himself up one day."

Confused, Violet said, "For what?"

Pushing off with his shoulder, Raddix stood to his full height. "Parents are so dense."

"Pardon me?" she mocked a flabbergasted tone.

He swallowed. "Although both you and my dad think you are fooling the town, you're not. Everyone sees you're both interested. Dad's fighting my mom's ghost."

Feeling guilty and exposed, Violet cut in before he could say another word. "I've never asked him to forget your mom, or—"

"Relax, it's my old man's issue. The question you need to answer is how long will you wait for him to win that fight?"

Her heart sank. *Forever.*

Violet had exhausted every other way to convince Sean she was ready to embark on a relationship with him. Either Sean made a move today, or she'd grab him by the back of the neck and kiss him hard, making him wonder why they hadn't kissed before now.

The mere thought had Violet's blood rushing through her veins.

She'd never try to replace Sara, or make Sean forget her, but asking her to keep her feelings dormant any longer bordered on torture.

She needed one thing: courage. Violet spent her time judging Sean's lack of action, but where had she been?

Until now, it never occurred to Violet to take the lead. She was used to the man chasing the woman he desired.

Heat crawled up her neck, and doubt settled on her chest, crushing her ribcage. "What if everyone is wrong and Sean is being a gentleman? It's possible for a man to be nice to women."

"Yeah, you've met me, right?" Raddix laughed and huffed out a breath as he mentioned Damon, Jeff, and Quinton as well.

She laughed as Raddix rattled off the men from the ranch, who were sweet on their women, but borderline grumps to everyone else. "Touché."

Her love for her late husband, Marcus, was immense. After navigating the grieving steps, she now craved happiness. Even though she still loved Marcus, spending time with Sean showed her that her heart had more to give.

If Raddix was right, and Sean was interested, maybe he needed a little push. She wondered if she could break through his shell, awakening the hibernating man.

For years, Violet longed for change but clung to her familiar loneliness, as it was less scary than sharing her emotions and being rejected.

Her best friend Myrtle, one-third of the Troublesome Trio, had been encouraging her to join a dating app for people in their forties and fifties.

Not. Going. To. Happen.

The single, available men in Haven Ridge were rare as hen's teeth. Most cowboys were in their thirties or younger. The gentlemen her age had significant others.

Except for Sean.

"You're good for him. I hope he sees that soon," Raddix admitted.

Her eyes mist.

"Don't do that! Remember, I'm a grinch if you're not Lily," He said, crossing his arms over his chest.

Violet blinked, drying up the moisture. "You're not fooling me, Raddix Lawrence. Lily has softened you."

Raddix blushed, waving off the comment. "Make yourself comfortable, Violet, and I'll check on my dad, so he doesn't miss Tanner's event."

"Thank you." Violet smiled and proceeded to the living room, where she heard hoots and hollers.

Since Violet had her heart set on Sean, she'd devoted her time and energy to show him she cared. Hopefully,

A short while later, multiple conversations were in full throttle. Violet tried to keep up, but her mind always drifted back to Sean. A text message she'd received from Myrtle—a new adventure for the septuagenarian—hadn't helped.

How's the hunky cattleman?

Fine.

No one ever gave the Troublesome Trio any free information, yet they unveiled people's secrets faster than the bronc rider on TV lost his grip, being disqualified this round.

Any kissing yet?

Violet wished.

No.

You are kidding! The girls and I can't do everything. We had you in each other's arms. Stop wasting these opportunities.

The mention of the dance a couple months back when Hazel conducted her own square dance knock off made Violet blush as she remembered Sean's muscular arms.

Sean's musky scent branded her nostrils that evening. She spent two and a half minutes gripping his biceps, wishing the song lasted longer. Even though he wore a long-sleeved flannel, it left little for the imagination as it clung to his arms and stretched across his chest.

Her icy fingers pressed against her flushed face. *Goodness!* A single memory brought her to life, like Frosty the Snowman when the kids put the hat on his head. Sadness hit her next when she realized she hadn't been in his arms since that dance.

"Violet, is this your first time watching Nationals?" Damon asked, distracting her from a whirl of emotions assaulting her.

"On T.V., yes. Marcus and I traveled to Las Vegas many times for the full ten days, but it's been a minute since I've watched."

She would not admit that she'd rather read than watch television. Her romance books are her constant companion. It sounded sad, but they kept Violet hopeful she and Sean could still have a happy ending.

Harlyn motioned to the TV. "Isn't it hard to watch in person? I can only imagine the distractions for the spectators and athletes."

"That's part of the charm, as the spectator, of course. Damon, you might disagree having competed."

Damon nodded. "It's a thrilling experience for sure."

Her stomach growled, alerting everyone that she hadn't eaten lunch after church in a pathetic attempt to rush here to see Sean. "Sorry."

"No worries." Amelia waved her hand, dismissing Violet's apology. "Does anyone know how long Sean and Raddix are going to be?"

Everyone looked at Violet. *Shoot!* Raddix had said her feelings were noticeable. "I have no idea."

She swallowed the lump in her throat when Amelia suggested they start eating without them.

Violet had waited for Sean this long. Even the simple task of eating without him soured her stomach.

"You go ahead. I'll wait for Sean," Violet said, hoping she didn't have to say that much longer.

Chapter 4

"Seriously, Sara, what am I supposed to do?" Sean scuffed his foot in the snow, wishing he'd put his jacket on to keep his flannel from getting drenched with accumulating snowflakes.

Speaking to Sara gave Sean the peace he needed to live a functional life. Thankfully, his brother Jack helped him get to this point after he helped raise Raddix when he was only five.

Sean will never forget his brother's tough love: *I'm sorry that Sara's gone, but Raddix isn't. God allowed you to save him for a reason. Get right with God again. Talk to your wife every day if you want, but move on.*

Two out of three isn't bad. Sean rededicated himself to the Lord right after his brother rebuked his poor behavior, and he'd talked to Sara every day.

But move on. How? Even though he'd recognized the crackling of electricity between him and Violet, he'd ignored it, honoring his dedication to Sara.

"I have no business thinking of Violet in any way other than the florist who helps me remember you," Sean rasped, swallowing his emotion.

"Is that what you think?"

Sean's eyes flashed toward the familiar voice. "What are you doing here?"

"Checking on you since you dashed out of the house like. . ." Raddix's voice trailed off. Analogies with houses on fire or escaping houses never went over well with Sean.

Early spring, thirty years ago, lightning struck a tree, and it fell through their home, crushing Sara instantly. Sean almost didn't find Raddix, who'd been knocked unconscious. By the grace of God, Raddix's little voice whimpered, alerting Sean to his whereabouts. Sean ran out of the house, Raddix wrapped in his arms, just before a fire sparked, catching the cabin on fire.

"Dad, you're human. Mom would understand," Raddix said, pursing his lips together and nodding.

Sean turned his back to his son. "I'm not discussing this with you," Sean said with a bite as he stuffed his hands in his jean pockets.

Raddix stepped forward in silence. Resting his hand on his dad's nearest shoulder. "Punishing yourself won't bring her back."

"I know," Sean said, gruff and low, crossing his arms and bowing his head.

"Then why not live?"

"Because I don't deserve to," Sean muttered. "If I couldn't save your mom, why should I get to enjoy life?"

"I thought someone named God decided who lived and died." Raddix pushed out something that resembled a laugh and crossed his arms, challenging his dad's stance.

"God left you here for a reason. I can't imagine it was only to work with the cattle." Sean glared at his son. "Though you're great at what you do," Raddix continued, not wanting to upset his dad, "there's more to life than your bovines."

Since Sara had died, working with cattle is all that Sean did. It's only since Lily came into Raddix's life that Sean started branching out beyond the ranch. She'd had private conversations with Sean that even Raddix didn't know the details.

"I know you're right. Lily always says the same thing, but I have obligations to Amelia, the ranch, and you. I can't focus on another woman."

Raddix's arm dropped, and he stepped in front of his dad. "First off, I'm a grown man. I'm not a child who needs to be taken care of. Besides, I'm married. You don't take care of me anymore," the corner of his lips curled up, "Lily does."

Sean held up his hand, not wanting to hear how Lily takes care of him.

"It sounds like excuses. No one questions your work ethic. Amelia respects you and not because you're her uncle. Haven't you noticed she asks your opinion a lot? Remember when Uncle Jack died? She wanted to get rid of the tractor, even though it was only two years old. You convinced her not to by telling her that her dad would want her to be smart with her financial decisions. Buying a new tractor because she couldn't stand to look at the machine that crushed her dad wasn't a good financial decision," he finished.

A wave of understanding flowed through Sean's mind. "So you're saying I'm using excuses to avoid moving on in life?"

"Yeah."

Sean glanced at his son, then back at Sara's gravestone.

"It's time to move on, Dad. That's what mom would want," Raddix voice, gentle and encouraging.

A blend of grief and sadness mixed with anticipation and joyful spirits as he thought of his past with Sara, and the potential future awaiting him. Thinking of Violet waiting at the ranch sent nerves racing through his stomach.

"You don't have to get married again, or anything else you don't want to, but it's obvious to the entire town that Violet is interested in you. It seems you enjoy spending time with her, too, so just start there. Two people keeping each other company."

Raddix paused, his words registering with his dad. "Besides, isn't marriage 'until death do you part'? Biblically speaking, you've been punishing yourself unnecessarily for a long, long time."

"I hear you, Son. Thank you."

Raddix smirked. "No problem. It feels good to be the one lecturing you."

"Get outta here," humor sounded in Sean's voice. "I need another minute. Please, let Violet know I'll be in soon."

The two hugged. A real hug, not one of those manly one armed hugs. No, Sean felt this embrace throughout. They hadn't done that since Raddix was a little boy.

As Raddix walked away, Sean stared at Sara's plaque. The falling snow picked up even more, drenching his flannel.

"Sara. I've loved no one as much as I do you."

He kneeled on the snowy ground and brushed off the stone. "I'll never forget you, but Raddix is right. It's time for me to move on. I'm going to try if it's okay."

Sean, standing tall, squeezed his eyes shut, desperately hoping to hold back the tears threatening to spill.

A biting breeze ran through Sean, but it left him with a calming peace he hadn't felt since Sara died. This was the sign he needed.

Chapter 5

R addix had returned at least ten minutes ago. He wasn't a man of many words, just like his dad, but he gave her a simple nod and smile, giving Violet hope things might progress with Sean.

Meanwhile, everyone else focused on the screen.

"Tanner is up next," Damon yelled toward the kitchen, and a herd of cowboys and their wives barreled into the living room.

Violet stood. "Should I go get Sean, so he doesn't miss it?"

"I'm here." He nodded toward her, and his soft gaze made Violet's stomach flip-flop.

His waterlogged flannel clung to his arms, showcasing his reward for years of manual labor.

Her breath hitched when he unbuttoned it, peeled it off, and draped it over a hook to dry. His t-shirt underneath latched onto his biceps, strangling them.

She forced her eyes away before she had to fan herself, revealing to everyone her desire for the cowboy.

One might mistake Sean for someone in his late thirties or forties based on his physique. The few light streaks of grey near his temple announced the golden years he'd entered. Violet wouldn't complain.

"Here's what you've been waiting for, folks." The TV announcer grabbed their attention. "Can Tanner Brooks grab the gold again this year?"

The living room erupted with cheers.

"Don't forget about Meadow. She's outshined every other horse in this competition." The screen flashed to the men on their horses trotting around the arena, warming up.

The excitement in Violet's stomach resembled snow flurries, but it blossomed into a snow squall when Sean's shoulder grazed hers as he passed in front of her. They stood next to each other, a moment passing. Violet could feel the weight of his lingering stare.

Don't say anything stupid.

Rather than focus on how she could feel Sean's body heat radiating from him, her laser focus rested on the words 'Previously Recorded' in the bottom left corner of the TV.

"I'm sorry if I upset you," she whispered, hoping that everyone's attention on the sporting event kept them enthralled, giving her a semi-private moment with her cowboy.

Her cowboy? Ha! *From my thoughts to your ears, Lord.*

Sean motioned for Violet to sit on the couch. He joined her, and their legs brushed against each other, sending goosebumps to her skin's surface. Then he straightened out his legs and crossed his ankles, leaving her skin rejected and cold.

Leaning over, he whispered, "You have nothing to be sorry about. Maybe after this, we could grab a cup of coffee and chat for a little while."

Violet's stomach hollowed out, and her heart bucked out of control like the horse on the TV. She felt heat emitting from her cheeks, but she prayed Sean hadn't noticed.

"That would be nice."

They sat there for the next few minutes, shoulders touching, and her nerves got the best of her. Violet's leg started bouncing up and down. *What could Sean want to talk about that he'd have to set it up like a date?*

This wasn't a date. He just wanted to talk and drink coffee. What had he and Raddix discussed?

Sean's calm demeanor gave nothing away. With his muscular arms crossed over his chest, he continued to watch the highlights of the other bronc riders.

Please, Lord, grant me peace that passes understanding with Sean, so I don't ruin anything that might be brewing.

Violet had never had any children, and she was an only child, so the crowd shocked her. Overtime, she'd grown fond of everyone at Big L' Ranch and wondered if she'd ever become part of this group as Sean's significant other.

The screen now showed Tanner behind a gate, and with a quick nod, cowboys opened that gate and Meadow bursts from the stall.

"You get your feet up there, Tanner," Damon hollered.

"Were his feet over Meadow's shoulders?" Emmanuel asked Damon with excitement.

"They looked it to me."

Sean leaned forward, resting his elbows on his knees, eyes glued to the screen.

Meadow bucked. Her high kick hit the mark.

"Yes!" Damon hollered.

"Perfect change of direction," he continued.

Everyone stood, holding their breath for the last few seconds.

Then the pick up rider arrived.

Tanner leaned his upper body over the back of the horse parallel to him and this round was complete.

"Yes!" the kids jumped and yelled.

"That's not good," Damon said, rubbing his hand down his face.

Violet was too preoccupied side glancing at Sean. She hadn't seen what happened, causing her excitement to deflate faster than a knife to an inner tube.

"He twisted his ankle on that the dismount. Hopefully, he can brush it off before tomorrow's round."

Everyone was talking at once. Violet's eyes bounced back and forth between everyone, trying to take it all in.

"Shh. Quiet. Tanner's on," Sean announced.

"Well, Tanner Brooks. That was an impressive ride. Were you trying to show off with your mark out?"

That Tanner Brooks smirk everyone at Big L' Ranch had grown accustomed to spread across his clean-shaven face.

"Not showing off. I'm giving the fans the best show possible since this is going to be my last competition."

Silence fell in the living room and everyone's head turn toward Damon, who shrugged. "He told me not to say anything."

"So it's important for you to walk out of here with another gold buckle."

"That's always the goal, otherwise why bother? But I have a gig all set up back in Haven Ridge, Montana. I get to work with animals and the people are pretty good, too." Tanner winked, making everyone laugh.

"But if I don't get gold. It'll be okay. I'll be upset, but I won't let a gold buckle define my worth. Thanks, Sean," Tanner said, pointing into the camera.

All heads turned toward Sean this time, yet he remained silent, per usual.

"Well, there you have it, folks. Tanner Brooks is retiring after Nationals here in Las Vegas. And it looks like he's well on his way to that gold buckle with his first score coming through: eighty-nine. Way to go, Tanner!" The announcer slapped the bronc rider's back.

Hoots and hollers erupted in the living room. Excitement took over Violet, and she threw her arms around Sean's waist in an enthusiastic hug.

After a long second, Sean returned it, warming her shoulders when he engulfed her petite frame.

She molded into his arms like she belonged there. Violet let herself relax. The words *permanent residency* flashed through her mind too quick as Sean jerked away.

Feeling embarrassed, Violet grabbed the closest items—two chips bowls with only crumbs scattered on the bottom—and announced, "I'll bring these to the kitchen and wash them out."

It surprised Violet that Sean had given Tanner sound advice. Perhaps she could ask him about that when they chat. If she was lucky, Sean would be ready to heed his own wisdom.

Chapter 6

The smell of coffee and french fries knocked Sean over when he pulled the diner door open and gestured for Violet to enter.

Sean needed to stay away from coffee right now. His mind raced, fueled by a gnawing anxiety that refused to relax.

The Troublesome Trio huddled in their corner, most likely planning *coincidences* for their next victims.

Raddix shared that the sheriff and Willow might have feelings for each other. *Lucky them!* Of course, no one either confirmed or denied these allegations since that would be more fuel for these ladies.

Myrtle waved, a coy smile plastered on her face, as Violet and Sean settled into a small booth on the other side of the diner, returning her smiling.

In another time and place, Sean would have turned on his heels and disappeared, hoping the trio forgot they saw him. He already had Raddix telling him what an idiot he'd been. Sean didn't need to hear it again.

When Violet sat, Sean contemplated sitting next to her since she slid in more than one would expect if sitting by themselves, but that seemed a little forward.

Instead, Sean sat across from her, wanting to focus on his message. His world stilled when disappointment or concern washed over her features.

Did she want me to sit next to her?

If Sean was being honest with himself, dread filled his gut, wishing he hadn't caused Violet's expression. Hopefully, Raddix was right, and Violet's mood would change when he shared his feelings with her.

Sean had enjoyed watching Nationals with Violet earlier today. After the way their legs rested against each other and how their shoulders touching sent little sparks throughout Sean's body, sitting across from her now left him greedy for more.

The new waitress, Frank and Hazel, hired a couple of days ago, stopped at their table.

"Hello. Can I get you something to drink?"

Before they could answer, Myrtle, Doris, and Hazel were at the table, too. A sense of unrest settled in Sean's stomach.

What plan do these ladies have for us? Sean wondered silently.

"Annika, these are my friends, so they'll be easy to start with."

Start with?

Violet smiled at the young woman. "I'm Violet. I own the flower shop across the street."

"Annika, commutes, taking her about an hour to get to work."

Sean knew what was coming next. No one had filled the apartment above the flower shop since Lily moved out.

This young woman must be in her late twenties or early thirties. She seemed skittish, like a filly, when Myrtle talked about her personal life.

"That's a shame." Violet's eyes sparkled, Sean knowing what she'd do next.

This woman was remarkable—always willing to help others. She never even asked background questions. If she got a positive feeling about the person, she let them rent.

Violet's method had worked in Raddix's favorite. Had Violet known a dangerous stalker was after Lily, she may not have let her stay and Raddix would have never fallen in love with her.

What was he saying? Of course, Violet would have insisted Lily stay and have police protection, too.

"It's the only place I can find for my son and his dog. And it's close to his school." Annika explained.

Violet smiled. "Schooling's out of my hands, but I have an apartment to rent. You could walk to work and save a lot of money on gas."

"That's rather generous of you," Annika began, "but Jackson's school has an after-school program that accepted him. I can't work without it."

Sean stuck out his hand. "Hi, I'm Sean. At Big L' Ranch, Reneé home-schools all the kids on the ranch. I'm sure she'd be willing to help you out if you wanted to make a home here."

What was I thinking? Reneé may kill me when she finds out I offered homeschooling to a complete stranger.

He couldn't help himself. Violet's warm and inviting spirit spread to everyone around her. Maybe this young woman wouldn't take them up on their offers.

The woman's eyes darted between Hazel, Doris, and Myrtle's, whose encouraging eyes were enough to convince anyone. But Sean's attention fell on Violet's green beauties.

Oh, no. Annika seemed to be pondering this idea. Should he take back the offer before she answered?

No! That would be awful. Violet is barely containing her excitement, hoping she'd found a renter, and Sean was sweating bullets hoping Annika declined.

"Yeah, I think that sounds wonderful. As long as we're not an inconvenience."

Violet hopped in her seat. *She is adorable.* "No imposition at all." She turned toward Sean with a bright smile. "You may want to give Reneé a heads up though."

Violet knew Sean had put his foot in his mouth, yet she encouraged Annika to say yes with her big smile and welcoming eyes. Looked like Sean wasn't the only one who couldn't resist Violet's goodness.

Sean pulled out his phone and texted Reneé. "What grade is Jackson in?" Sean looked at Annika for her answer.

"He's in fourth."

Sean focused on his phone, hoping Reneé didn't respond right away, and simultaneously prayed she did, so the tongue lashing he prepared himself for could be over quickly.

"I'll let you know what Reneé says," Sean commented and placed his phone face down on the table.

"Okay. Thank you so much. While we wait, how about I take your order?" She pulled out her notepad and pencil.

Violet ordered first when Sean gave her a quick nod. "I'll have a coffee and a slice of Hazel's apple pie. Thank you."

For a second, Sean stared at the woman who just ordered dessert. He'd heard that most women wouldn't order food, let alone a dessert when out with a man. Pride bubbled to the surface, glad that Violet felt comfortable enough with him to order junk food.

"I'll have the same," he announced proudly, and then felt like a dummy for sounding that way.

What is coming over me? Lord, don't let me be an idiot.

"Sure thing. I'll be right back with your coffee," Annika had a little hop to her step that he hadn't noticed before.

"Thank you, Violet," Hazel said as she slid in next to the kind woman, and hugged her like she hadn't seen her in years.

"No problem. You know me. I'm happy to help when I can."

"Come on Hazel," Doris announced while Myrtle jerked her head toward Sean.

These women were anything but subtle, making Sean chuckle and clear his throat.

Once the ladies retreated to their corner, Sean almost wished they would return. He didn't know where to start. What if he put himself out there and Violet didn't reciprocate?

Breathe. He steeled himself. He'd just witnessed her kindness toward people. How could he doubt her sincerity? What if she was merely extending a hand of friendship? Violet was also a business owner. Would she be anything but helpful to one of her best customers?

Never.

Sean twisted in his seat and stretched his arms across the table, almost like he was reaching for Violet's hands. Earlier today, he convinced himself to tell Violet he saw her as more than just his florist. Right now, he'd decided even faster to mute himself.

Violet stared out the window with a yearning look.

"Snow is so beautiful. I just don't like driving in it," Violet gave him an insight into her thoughts.

It'd started snowing again when they'd arrived at the diner fifteen minutes ago, and now the blizzard-like conditions swirled outside their window, keeping Violet preoccupied. *Thank you, God!*

"I'm glad I'll be taking you home tonight." Sean gulped when he realized how that sounded. *Here we go again.* Sean shook his head.

"I mean driving you home. . . your home. . . and dropping you off. Then I'll go home to my place."

"Well, Sean Lawrence, flustered twice in one day. I'm starting to feel special," Violet said with an amused tone.

If you only knew. If Sean could drop his guard, he might not be flustered any more.

He ran his hand along his jaw, reminding him that he hadn't shaved today. "Apparently, I have an easier time interacting with cattle than humans."

"Is that supposed to be a compliment or a slam? I've never been compared to cattle before." Violet mocked being offended. Her playful tone put Sean at ease.

"You definitely smell better than the cattle," he tried to fix his blundering words, and slapped his palm to his face and dragged his hand down, gripping his throat, as if he were trying to choke himself with one hand.

Violet moved her hands from the table for Annika to place their coffee mugs and carafe in the center. "Do you want cream and sugar?"

"No thank you," Violet responded in unison with Sean's, "Yes, please."

Annika placed those items in front of Sean. As Violet reached for the carafe, Sean's hand covered hers, and the sparks tickled his palm. "Let me."

"Thank you." The pink on her cheeks was adorable.

"Your pie should be ready in a few minutes," Annika said with a cheery tone and returned to the kitchen.

Sean filled Violet's cup and then his own. He poured cream and scooped three teaspoons of sugar into his cup and stirred.

Now that he had something to keep his hands busy, maybe he could calm down.

Their eyes met. "I know. I use too much sugar and cream."

"No judgment." Violet shook her head and smiled, sipping her drink.

The second hand on the wall clock alerted him that his time was running out. If he wasn't going to tell Violet how he felt, why did he bring her here?

They sat there sipping their coffee until she broke the silence.

"So, are you going to tell me what you wanted to chat about, or are you going to keep me guessing?"

Violet's bluntness stirred up memories of Sara, reminding Sean of the quality she found most attractive in his late wife, and the woman sitting across from him.

The moment of truth gave Sean pins and needles. Grinding his feet into the floor, his thighs burned. Sean hands squeezed the porcelain coffee cup, praying it didn't combust in his hands. He needed to put himself out there and risk rejection or stay silent forever. His life had been mundane and full of work until Violet arrived and threw everything into disarray.

Talking with Violet when he picked up Sara's flowers had turned into the brightest part of his day. He didn't want that to end if this got awkward.

Sean looked around the diner, but not for a person. Aside from the Troublesome Trio and Annika, the diner was empty. He was stalling. His nerves were always on display, and now was no different. Sweat bubbles started forming at his hairline.

Violet reached out, placing her soft palm on his forearm. Which he clenched instinctively when her touch shot an electric current all the way to this shoulder.

"I need to apologize for running out this morning." Yeah. That was the perfect place to start. Her reaction would tell Sean how much he could share.

Violet's brows raised. "You have nothing to be sorry for. In fact, I thought I said something to upset you, so I planned on apologizing to you."

Sean had heard it all. A woman willing to apologize to a man. He just may be in love.

Chapter 7

"Violet, dear, this is wonderful," Myrtle cooed one snowy morning at the flower shop. "These wreaths will be perfect for the town Christmas party."

Violet blew off the compliment. Myrtle was always gushing over her work. While Violet appreciated it, she wasn't feeling festive or inspired at the moment, so she wondered if she should put her wreath making on hold for now.

It had been six days since she'd spoken with Sean. He hadn't even come in for his weekly bouquet for Sara's gravesite. The thought sat like an anchor in her stomach, preventing her from eating more than a bird all week.

In this time, she'd helped Annika, her son, Jackson, and his dog Brewster get settled into the apartment. She'd taken them to the ranch to meet Reneé and the kids, hoping to see Sean, but he hadn't appeared in the three hours they were there. He was avoiding her, but she didn't know why.

Violet had watched Nationals on her own even though Raddix had invited her to the ranch. She didn't want her presence to make Sean feel uncomfortable in his own home.

Tanner was in the lead. He and Meadow hadn't scored less than eighty-seven points on any round. He had three days left to hold on to and grow his lead.

Violet recognized how much work it took to manage the cattle at the ranch, and Sean was watching Tanner, so she kept telling herself his absence had nothing to do with her. If only she could believe herself.

"Are you sure you're okay?" Myrtle asked, putting the wreath down.

Violet let out a frustrated sigh. "I'm fine."

"Honey, you're talking to me. Any woman who says she's fine is the exact opposite." Myrtle's boisterous voice filled the shop.

"We've been friends too long for me to think you're okay," Myrtle continued, following Violet around the store at a much slower pace.

Violet's face softened. "I've got all these wreaths to make and I can't bring myself to focus on getting them done. Sean hasn't contacted me since he dropped me off last week. I thought he wanted to talk about going on a real date, or something that would show there was a man living within that body."

Myrtle narrowed her eyes at Violet. "Is that all that's bothering you? I can fix that easily."

"Don't you dare, Myrtle." Violet dropped the boughs. "That's why I haven't said anything."

Violet felt her cheeks warm as she remembered the tenderness Sean showed her when he dropped her off. He opened her door and engulfed her little hand in his masculine one, making sure she didn't slip on any ice hiding underneath the newly fallen snow.

When they reached her door, he held out his hand. "May I?" he asked, reaching for her keys.

After he unlocked the door, he opened it, turned on the light, and escorted her into the entryway.

"Would you like me to check things out before I leave?"

How could someone act so concerned for her safety and then avoid contact for a week?

She'd walked into her house many times all by herself. She turned on lights, checked doors, closed curtains. Same routine, four years since Marcus died.

But her heart soared like a helium balloon when Sean did this for her. The simple gesture showed he cared, and that meant more to Violet than all the success at her shop.

Myrtle's hawk eyes were examining Violet's facial expression. "Something happened, didn't it?" she asked, pulling Violet from her recollection.

No! She wanted to scream, but didn't, not wanting to upset Myrtle. All she could think about was the hug Sean wrapped her in before he left, pressing his powerful upper body against her.

Her head rested against the middle of his chest and he kissed the top of Violet's head, lingering long enough suggesting an affectionate couple. When he pulled away from the hug, his dark eyes promising a better kiss awaited.

Violet's hands remembered the muscles underneath his signature flannel that night, which seemed like decades ago. She'd dragged her hands long along his sides and gripped his shirt until it became awkward, realizing he would not kiss her again.

"Something's going to happen," Myrtle huffed, pulling Violet back to the present.

Violet lifted a brow. "If Sean wants nothing to do with me, I'm not pushing myself on him."

Myrtle stared at her in silence, her brain already plotting something. That was never a good sign. A slow smile grew on Myrtle's face, and Violet could only fathom what her friend had in store for her.

At seventy something, Myrtle's keen personality resembled that of a twenty-year-old. "Sean Lawrence won't know what hit him when we're through."

Great! If he doesn't hate me now for some inconceivable reason, once the Troublesome Trio deals with him, he will forget all about me for sure.

Chapter 8

Christmas was a heartbeat away. Kids would be free to help set up for the party at the end of the week.

They decided on a Santa's workshop decorative theme. Reneé was the perfect teacher for the kids on the ranch. She had them creating the banners and decorations during their art classes.

Carolyn and Cash, the ranch chefs, would bake gingerbread cookies for the decorating contest, and make all the finger foods for guests to enjoy.

Amelia and Quinton would give sleigh rides along the property, while Damon would oversee pony rides, and Raddix would let the kids try feeding their newest calf during the day.

Reneé and Lily were in charge of the craft table. They had foam Christmas trees, candy canes, and manger scenes to assemble. Kids could take the crafts with them once they finished them.

Willow would set up a Christmas card creation table. Here, people could make cards for shut-ins and those who parishioners requested receive a little extra love during the holidays.

Raddix decided a "snowball" pit in one corner would be the perfect addition to the party.

"It's for the kids," he argued.

Lily dragged her hand along his upper back and rested her head on his shoulder. "No need for excuses. You can play in the snowball pit, too." She laughed and kissed him on the cheek.

Raddix smacked her bottom as she walked away, leaving a longing in Sean's chest. He missed Violet.

If he'd told her how he felt, Violet might be here right now, helping plan the party.

"I'll paint some of those plastic ball pit balls white to resemble snowballs. The kids will love throwing them at each other."

"Raddix, only you would think of that, but I have to admit, it sounds like a solid plan," Amelia said, shaking her head.

Turning her attention to the meeting host, Amelia announced, "If you're good with me, I need to get back to work." She stood and waited for Myrtle's confirmation.

Scanning her paperwork, Myrtle nodded. "All set, Amelia. Thank you."

How much longer will this take? I have cows to tend to. Sean wondered if he could escape with Amelia.

Sean was never rude to these ladies. Not only because they were his elders, but also because they were dangerous, in a grandma meddling in your business sort of way.

Hazel and Doris were speaking in hush tones, which scared him more than he'd admit aloud.

He didn't need to hear specifics. Sean knew they were up to their shenanigans again. "People won't like you intervening in their lives again."

"Don't be such a cynic, Sean." Doris dismissed his comment. "Single men and women want only one thing: to meet someone they're attracted to and see if they're a match."

Sean shook his head. "You might consider polling people. I think you are way off base."

Myrtle glowered at him before taking a breath and relaxing her features. "Just because you're not interested in any women in town doesn't mean other men won't snatch them up, leaving you in the dust." Her eyes narrowed as they fixed on him.

What did Myrtle know about his love interests?

Love? Sean shook his head. *No!*

Was he interested in Violet? Sure. He wasn't able to tell her, though. He'd tried the night he dropped her off after they had coffee and pie at the diner. That was an epic failure.

He'd kicked himself every day since that night. Once he'd wrapped his arms around her and pressed her soft curves against his chest and abs, he had the urge to pick her up and kiss her the rest of the night.

Instead, he chickened out. He kissed her on the top of the head and retreated. Since then, he hadn't contacted her. For the first time, he'd put flowers from Randall's convenience store on Sara's grave.

"What would you like me to help with, Myrtle?" Sean asked, trying to keep the meeting on track.

"I need two things from you. First, you'll need to help Violet with the wreaths she made for decoration and set up the other wreaths that are part of a silent auction. We're donating the proceeds to the church to help families in need."

Help Violet? Sean nodded. *Thank you, ladies.* "I can do that," Sean said with ease, hoping his excitement didn't radiate off him. "What's the other thing?"

The ladies glanced at each other before turning their attention to their papers. "It's a simple request," Myrtle stated with a smile, telling Sean it would be anything but simple.

Myrtle slid a picture toward the middle of the table.

No way!

Eyes locked, they sized each other up. Her piercing eyes were intimidating. *These women must hate me.* It's not like Sean hadn't done this before. Christmas time was about being generous with everything, including our time.

He sighed. "Okay, I'll do it."

Chapter 9

"I'll never finish in time," Violet fretted aloud to her empty shop, looking at loose boughs, decorations, and spools of ribbon scattered across her large workbench, normally meant for making flower arrangements.

For the last eight weeks, her wreath making supplies had taken over most of the bench, leaving only a corner for flower arrangements.

Feeling less creative than usual, Violet picked up a spool of ribbon, measured out a yard, and began making a bow. That was something she could do on autopilot—thinking wasn't necessary. *Thank God*! She'd had a difficult time with thinking about anything other than Sean since their coffee outing.

Sean called her about an hour ago, letting her know that he'd pick her up because it started snowing.

Sean had remembered that she didn't enjoy driving in the snow. Maybe she shouldn't be so eager to see Sean. But she was. Any attention from Sean and Violet felt like a giddy teenager again.

Stains marred her jeans, and strands of her hair were escaping her ponytail.

"If I don't stop working now, I'll never be ready," Violet said aloud.

Tonight was the last Saturday before Christmas, and the town's annual Christmas party. This year, Amelia and Quinton thought it would be fun to have it at their ranch where the kids could have some outdoor activities, too.

She would be lying if she said she wasn't thrilled about having alone time with Sean. All week she'd thought about going on a private sleigh ride with him.

Sadly, that sleigh dashed through the snow in the opposite direction of her and Sean. Violet's heavy eyelids reminded her she hadn't slept well all week. A tall, handsome, stand-offish cowboy had preoccupied her thoughts all day and night.

In true Myrtle fashion, she persuaded Sean to help her set up the wreaths around the ranch, but Violet hadn't spoken to Sean since their coffee outing.

What did I do wrong?

She spied the smaller wreath she'd made especially for him to put on Sara's grave and started doubting whether she should give it to him.

Knock, knock. Her time had run out.

She pressed her palms down the front of her shirt and down the flowy skirt she'd chosen for this evening. Her untouched hair would have to do, not that it would matter to him, anyway.

Pulling the door toward her, she lost her breath.

Before her, Sean stood his full height in a pair of dark blue jeans, dressy cowboy boots, his dressy cowboy hat, and one of his signature flannel shirts with the top button left undone.

His light hair, neatly cut, called my fingers to weave through it. His warm, sapphire eyes were soft and inviting, and a thin layer of stubble did little to cover his strong, square jawline. She drank him in, knowing that the memory of him that she'd been living with since she'd last seen him hadn't done him justice.

If it weren't for the doorknob taking the bulk of her weight, Violet would have been on the floor.

"H-hi," she muttered. "You look. . . *stunning, gorgeous, beautiful.* Would he mind being called any of those? The last thing she wanted to do was offend him the first time they'd seen each other in what felt like forever.

"Sexy," she finished, clasping her hand over her mouth.

Violet's insides shriveled like the Wicked Witch of the East's legs when Glinda removed the ruby slippers from her feet. The intense heat blazing up her neck burned high on her cheeks.

"I shouldn't say half of the things I think in my out loud voice," she said, dropping her hand and ducking her chin to hide her embarrassment.

"Oh, no," Sean smirked. "Feel free to say anything you're thinking about if it involves telling me how *sexy* I am."

Violet knew how humble Sean was, so he was only teasing her and enjoying it. She relished in this side of Sean—relaxed, open, and confident. It may be a fake confidence, she wasn't sure, but it was sexy nonetheless.

Sean cleared his throat. "You look stunning, Violet."

His words had Violet's insides squealing like a thirteen-year-old. She brought her hand to her face. If her warm cheeks were any indication, Sean had made her blush.

"May I come in?"

Violet stepped back. "Yes, of course." She shut the door once he cleared the threshold.

"The wreaths are in the back workshop."

She felt Sean on her heels, making her wish he would wrap his arms around her again, so she could feel his strength.

Of course, that didn't happen. They reached the long, wooden table with wreaths and materials to make more scattered about. Turning to face him, she once again lost her breath. His musky aftershave was crippling her defenses.

Who could resist a strong, handsome cowboy with powerful arms and a musky smell? Not Violet.

"It looks like Christmas exploded in here," Sean said with a grin.

"Yeah, I ran out of time. I'm three short for decorations, but we'll make it work."

Sean pointed to the baby wreath she'd made for him and asked, "Why is that one so small?"

Her cheeks reddened for the second time in a matter of minutes. "That's for you to put on Sara's grave."

He stared at her with a slackened jaw.

"Only if you want to," Violet said in a rush, feeling comfortable. "I'm not sure how large of a stone Sara has, but if you don't want it or like it, I understand. Don't feel obligated to use it. I know Randall has wreaths, too."

He winced. Violet was almost felt remorseful, hating that she put Sean on the spot about getting Sara's flowers at Randall's this week, but it was a small town. He knew people talked, and if he'd told me himself, they wouldn't be in this awkward place now.

"Thank you, Violet," he began and stopped, staring at her with an intensity and softness the same, making Violet wonder if he was happy or upset about the wreath.

The deafening silence worked on Violet's nerves. *Move on, Violet, and forget about growing any closer to this man. He's not interested.*

He made his feelings clear by ignoring her. They couldn't go back to their simple conversation making flower arrangements for Sara, or else they would have. Instead, Sean skipped their time together last week.

She reached for a wreath. "Maybe if you extend your arms, I can load the wreaths on you? That's the quickest way to get them to the truck," Violet said, breaking the silence and getting things back on track.

Sean stuck his arms out like Frankenstein. "Go for it. Cover me in green."

Violet suppressed a giggle as she imagined the Jolly Green Giant from vegetable cans when she was a kid as she started loading the wreaths on his outstretched arms.

Who was she kidding? The image of a green vegetable giant would never give justice to the man towering over her. Even covered in dirt and hay, his handsomeness knew no bounds.

With his arms full, he lowered his head. "I can take one more around the neck."

She secured it in place. As he lifted his chin, their gazes locked on one another, their mouths inches away. All she'd have to do was push onto her toes and let her full lips connect with his.

Their breath mingled together another second, then Sean straightened to his full height—making him way out of her reach.

What was she thinking? He'd made it clear he wasn't interested, but she was pushing herself on him, anyway. Apparently, age didn't matter; she was acting like a love-sick a teenager.

Her brain kept telling her to move on and not pay attention to Sean Lawrence, but her heart continued to play tug-a-war with her thoughts and every chance it got, her heart lead the way.

"You got any more?" he asked almost breathlessly.

"Nope. I hope those last ones didn't suffer from my rushing."

He scoffed playfully. "Please! Your work is as gorgeous as you."

Shock registered on his face.

Did he forget himself or is he really letting his true feelings show like a truth serum?

She rushed to the door, trying to avoid showing off her warm cheeks. Once he exited, she let out an enormous sigh as she closed the door.

Violet would have to dig deep and tell Sean how she felt. She couldn't imagine her life without him in it, but she may have to if Sean didn't have feelings for her. Violet opened the door and Sean was waiting there for her.

He looked as nervous as a boy picking up his high school prom date. That made her chuckle inwardly.

Grabbing her coat, she avoided eye contact with him, not sure what to make of his last comment. Then he surprised her again.

Sean hooked his finger under her chin, forcing her eyes to meet his. "I don't say things I don't mean," his voice, low and gravelly.

The air between them charged with jolts of electricity. Sean leaned down, wrapping his arms around her waist, pulling her flush to his chest.

Her breath caught in her throat, her eyes widening as she took in the imposing, powerful form before her. With her palms resting on his firm chest, she silently pleaded, *Please let him kiss me.*

Their lips, only centimeters apart, were about to connect. The kiss she'd been waiting for was about to happen.

Not yet.

His buzzing phone forced them apart. An audible sigh filled the air as he read the text and stuffed it back into his front pocket.

"Raddix, telling me to get back now." He offered his arm. "Ready?"

Violet wrapped her fingers around his biceps. Her heart swelled with contentment, understanding that this was all they needed for the moment. Their kiss would come. . . soon.

"I appreciate your willingness to help even though it must be hard for you," she broke the silence between them as they rode to the ranch.

Violet silently cheered herself on in her effort to be more direct. The unknown hung heavy in the air. If Sean wasn't looking for anything beyond a professional connection, she would have to accept it, but the current state of uncertainty was too much to bear.

It didn't matter how old you were; rejection still stung.

"It's not hard," he muttered. "You're a quick drive from the ranch. Besides, this helps out a lot of people."

The weight of his words hung in the air, a heavy silence that drowned out her own muddled thoughts.

One thing was for sure: he was sending mixed messages. The tender way he helped her into the truck by placing his hand on her lower back turned cold and impersonal now, leaving her with a hollow ache in her chest. She squeezed her eyelids tight, hoping they wouldn't escape.

The twenty-minute drive to the ranch was plenty of time to have a frank discussion, yet Violet lost her nerve and stared out the window, praying for God's direction.

Unfortunately, she hadn't stopped her silent prayers long enough to see if God had answered. Before she knew it, they were pulling into the driveway at Big L' Ranch and asked, "What time is everyone arriving?"

"One, but I'm sure some people will show early. That's how it always is," Sean answered, keeping his gaze forward.

The entire drive here, he'd kept his hands on the steering wheel, squeezing tight, clear by his white knuckles.

"Perfect. That gives me thirty minutes to set everything up."

Violet scrambled out the truck door, her frantic movements fueled by a desperate need for air.

Colossal mistake.

Violet slipped on the ice hidden under the freshly fallen snow the instant her feet hit the ground.

She stood just as Sean rounded the front of the truck. "Are you okay?"

"I'm good. Thank you."

He walked beside her to the barn. When Sean opened the door, joy flowed through Violet as she entered Santa's workshop. The room sparkled with tinsel the kids had hung everywhere–the tree, counters, and the end of the tables. They even glued tinsel, much to Reneé's chagrin, Violet imagined, on the banners.

Sean grazed her arm and fingers every time they hung the wreaths. Was he doing that on purpose? Violet hoped so, but it could be coincidental.

"Your hands are amazing." Sean stared down at her with dark eyes.

"They have their moments." Violet almost winced at her lame attempt to flirt.

Sean leaned closer. Was he going to kiss her? *Yes, please.* Her eyes dipped to his lips and back up to his dark, intense eyes.

Finally, Sean, the man of few words, would rather show her how he felt.

At the last second, he reached around her shoulder and grabbed one of the last wreaths they needed to hang.

Seriously!?

She was too old for this nonsense.

"Put this over the bathroom door." Violet shoved it at Sean's chest and grabbed the last wreath from the table before she stalked away.

Violet hung the last wreath over the hat rack in the entryway. A fleeting glance at Sean's face revealed a pain mirrored in her own heart. Their eyes locked. Her breath caught when he pulled the cowboy hat from his head and ran his fingers through his hair before he smashed it back on his head. His dark eyes called her name.

He brushed past her. "I need some air." The slamming door made Violet jump.

Fed up, she followed Sean into the dark night. The warm barn deceived her, making her forget that it was barely twenty degrees.

"Sean," he spun on his heels. She knew her gruff tone was out of character, but she didn't care at the moment.

"Go back inside. It's freezing and I have nothing to give you."

Ha! He had plenty to give, if he would be willing.

Toe to toe, she stared at him. "If you get mad at me, sorry, not sorry, but I'm tired of waiting for you. I can take rejection. . . but don't be too harsh."

Confusion splayed across his face. It wasn't until Violet linked her fingers behind his neck and bent him nearly in half that some semblance of understanding showed in his expression, and then she pressed her lips to his.

Chapter 10

It took a couple of seconds for Sean's brain to register what was happening.

For the past few months, Violet's eyes had lit up every time Sean spoke, warming his insides. His insecurities had robbed him of spending time with Violet this past week when he refused to communicate with her.

But right now, she was speaking his language. Sean drew her hips flush with his body. He pressed his fingertips tighter into her skin, hoping he wasn't being too rough. Then his hands roamed over her back, letting his fingers drift to her hair and weaved through her strands. He tilted her head with his free hand, deepening the kiss.

Why hadn't I done this earlier?

Slowing the kiss down so he could recapture a little oxygen—it'd been a long time since he'd kissed anyone; he'd have to work on his endurance.

His weathered fingers gently brushed the snowflakes from her shoulders and then captured her cheeks with what he hoped was more gentle than the tsunami of emotions thrashing through his chest.

He pulled back, searching Violet's eyes. Her sea-green beauties captivated him. His thoughts lingered in the air, bittersweet and tinged with ghosts of memories he'd buried deep. But in her eyes, he saw a reflection of his future with Violet.

His breath hitched as her gaze fell upon his lips. "If you are having second thoughts, say something now," his voice, low and breathy.

Violet worried her lip for a moment before shaking her head. "Never. I've been waiting for this for a long time." She pushed to her toes and pressed her soft lips against his, and he released a masculine noise from the back of his throat that even surprised him.

Violet's lips smiled against his.

"What? Do you enjoy torturing me?"

She held her lips against his for an exaggerated second. "Are you saying kissing me is torture?"

He pulled her away so he could see her face. His brow furrowed as he stared down at her. "No. The torture is having to stop."

A clatter inside the hall caused Violet to jump.

"I've got you," Sean declared, his voice full of warmth as he drew her in, his laughter echoing through the air.

She wrapped her arms about his waist, eliminating all the space between them. "Don't laugh at me."

"I'm sorry. I've seen no one jump that high before," he teased.

Laughter bubbled up inside her as Violet's hand connected with his biceps, a playful spark igniting a warm feeling within him. Her voice vibrated against his chest when she asked, "Sean, what did that kiss mean?"

Why did everything suddenly feel like a dark, looming shadow creeping closer, suffocating any sense of peace or safety out of Sean's lungs?

Women were difficult to understand. Why did everything have to mean something?

It had been a long time since Sean kissed a woman, so that *must* mean something.

What?

He wasn't sure.

Kissing a woman like that evoked a lot of other feelings for a man, and it might have been decades, but he knew better than to share those feelings with Violet.

"How about we just enjoy the night and talk about specifics later? The party is about to start."

Violet's body tensed and a knot tightened in his stomach, a reminder of his difficulty to get involved with a woman.

He drew her back and whispered, "Is that okay?" A chill ran down his spine when she answered, her voice laced with disapproval.

"That's fine."

Sean cringed. One thing he had learned was that whenever a woman said that, it usually meant the opposite.

He reached for her hand and she took at least three steps back and said, "I have to go finish the decorations before anyone else arrives. Thank you for your help earlier."

He could only watch, his stomach twisting with a desperate plea for a chance to make things right before the barn door sealed their fate. Sean never spoke, and Violet vanished.

Perhaps I'm not ready to be involved with a woman just yet.

Chapter 11

Enjoy the night? Talk later? He had no problem kissing me now, but he wants to talk later.

Violet muttered as she soared away from Sean. Those words sat like boulders on her chest.

Confusion swirled in her mind like a blizzard. Was Sean the enemy? She had walked away from him, leaving him standing alone in the air's chill, and the silence of her absence. She got a strong sense of Déjà vu, thinking of how Sean ignored her.

Her anger spiked when she asked in a hush whisper, "Who kisses a woman with such intensity and then pretends it's nothing?" He had another coming if he thought she'd be an *easy* catch.

"Violet!" Myrtle hollered as she scuffed her feet across the floor, shuffling toward her friend as quickly as possible.

She could already hear Myrtle's relentless voice in her ear, peppering her with questions and refusing to leave her alone. Even from afar, she could tell when Violet was upset by the way her shoulders slumped.

"That look means trouble for some guy," Myrtle chuckled, her words laced with sarcasm as she delivered the old joke.

Violet shook her head, determined not to paint Sean as a villain. "No trouble here."

"Nice try," Myrtle retorted when she finally reached Violet.

The woman's eyes narrowed, studying Violet like notes for a final exam. "You smell like cologne."

Heat slithered up Violet's neck. Before Violet could confirm or deny Myrtle's accusation, the keen woman continued. "Were you snuggling up to a certain cowboy?" Myrtle asked, whistling low and rubbing her hands together.

Yes! That kiss! Angels above sang songs about kisses like that.

For a man who, according to the rumors, hadn't dated another woman since his wife passed away, he possessed an unexpected skill in the art of kissing.

And that cologne! Violet didn't stand a chance.

"You were!" Myrtle screamed.

"Shhh." Violet escorted her friend to a chair.

"Tell me what happened."

Violet could die a happy and content woman if that kiss was the only Christmas present she got this year.

The way he took control. He put his hands in all the right places, causing Violet's goosebumps to breed more instantly.

"We kissed," she gushed in a hush tone, hoping word didn't spread around the barn like a high school.

Myrtle shook her head. "I figured that much. Why are you angry?"

The air thickened. Violet's insides trembled at the thought of how Sean had burrowed his way under her skin months ago. Dread loomed over her as the words *Sean is not available* ran through her mind.

But Violet hadn't heeded the warning. She couldn't help herself. The kiss, a desperate plea for connection, exposed her feelings for Sean, leaving her drenched in fear and uncertainty when he didn't reciprocate.

Had he rejected her? *No. He said they would discuss it later.* Violet had made a mistake.

She let out a light chuckle. "Everything's fine. I had too high expectations."

Violet's eyes combed the room, searching for Sean, the knot of frustration in her stomach dissolving. Demanding immediate answers from him because of her impatience was unfair. She needed to apologize for her actions when she saw him again.

"If you're talking about Sean Lawrence, your expectations are not high enough. He's been single for too long. It's about time he commits to a woman." Myrtle sounded annoyed, but Violet knew better.

"Don't worry about this," Violet dismissed the situation with a wave of her hand. "Look at the snow coming down. The kids are full of energy tonight," Violet said, looking out the window into the parking lot where children were scooping up snow and throwing it at the person nearest them.

What Violet wouldn't give to be a carefree child again.

Before too long, the party was well underway. Myrtle, a whirlwind of mischief, found her group of friends and was devising schemes for unsuspecting couples all over Haven Ridge.

Kids were throwing the snowballs Raddix created at each other in rapid succession, with Raddix at the helm of that mission.

Reneé snagged Violet early on for assistance at the craft table. The kids had big hearts. They'd already made so many cards for others. One little girl from a town over was making a small wreath for her grandmother's grave, so Rocco, Reneé's husband and the ranch's veterinarian helped her, while Violet tended to the wreath maker.

The colorful banners and swirls hanging all around Santa's Workshop showcased the kid's love of the season and this annual event. Even Jackson connected with the kids.

When she'd arrived, kids were twirling garland around posts and draping it in half moons in front of each table. A few decorations sagged, but the garland the kids hung with Jeff held onto the festive atmosphere. Still fresh in her mind, Violet smiled at the memory of them earlier.

"Uncle Jeff, can I get on the ladder to hang that?" Emmanuel asked, rubbing his fingers together and bouncing on the balls of his feet.

"Yep. It's your turn."

Emmanuel's lips flicked briefly, but tugged back into a straight line.

"I'll hold the ladder," Darlene said, all smiles and cheery, as Jeff guided her friend to the ladder.

"Why don't you hand the garland to him?" Jeff suggested.

She rolled her eyes at her self-proclaimed uncle. "I guess so, but that's baby work."

Violet's eyes met Jeff's, and they shared a chuckle. She didn't envy Damon heading into teenage years with a girl. Darlene had enough sass for a whole cheering squad. Fortunately, he had people like Jeff and his wife, Katy, to help.

More than a dozen sprigs of mistletoe hung all around the barn. At first, though, she figured it had been Emmanuel's doing, but then she noticed three short, but elderly elves hanging them on their own fruition. That didn't put Violet's mind to rest any easier.

Who were they trying to capture under the mistletoe? The intensity of her first kiss with Sean had left Violet breathless, and she wasn't sure she could handle another one.

Besides, before she could get Sean under the mistletoe, Violet has to apologize. Had he left? Since she stormed away, Sean had been MIA. The longer she went without apologizing, the harder it would be.

Chapter 12

"I can't believe I agreed to this," Sean muttered, stuffing his foot into the last boot.

At least he could make the kids happy this evening since he'd already ruined Violet's. Unintentionally, of course.

He threw the red, velvet sack over his shoulder and slipped out the back door when he heard Reneé announce the reading of a famous Christmas story.

Outside, he met Raddix, who was on the roof, preparing to cause a clatter just like the Night Before Christmas story declared.

Screams from inside let Sean know Raddix had been successful. He whipped open the door and his in deep baritone voice, he bolstered, "HO, HO, HO, Merry Christmas!"

When he entered the room, kids scurried from the left and right until they surrounded him like a pack of wolves ready to pounce. He wondered if he should drop the sack of gifts and run for his life. Not really.

He scanned the room, hoping to find Violet. It'd crushed him, knowing he upset her.

Finally, he found her cleaning the craft table. Their eyes met. Her eyes softened, letting him know she'd let her guard down. That gaze. It sent a warm sensation through his lower belly.

She marched towards him, her jaw clenched tight, the cacophony of children's voices fueling his anticipation. Sean's face flushed with excitement, his heart pounding in rhythm with the joyful melody of the Christmas music playing in the background. The fire in her eyes, the promise of adventure burning bright, ignited a spark of excitement within him.

"Santa, where's Mrs. Claus?" A little tyke, about four, asked Sean, throwing him even more off kilter.

Frozen. His brain and mouth could not function.

"She's back at the North Pole, right Santa?" Violet answered for him, giving him an assuredly look.

Sean blinked. "That's right. In fact, I have to hurry. She's got my cookies and milk ready. HO, HO, HO," he pushed out.

As he reached into the present sack and pulled out a gift, Violet sidled beside him. "Would you like some help?" she asked, barely above a whisper.

"Please." Was it wrong to think of her as *his* Mrs. Claus? Probably, but that was where Sean's mind drifted.

They worked as one–Violet passing Sean the gift from the bag and him giving it, along with a candy cane, to each child.

A wave of courage filled his chest when their fingers brushed against each other again, and he whispered in her ear, "May I drive you home?"

She tucked a strand of hair behind her ear as she reached way down for one of the last gifts. "You were my ride here, so you better not desert me."

Sean sniggered, but only for a moment, trying to stay in character. A rush of excitement flooded his belly at the idea of embracing Violet. This Christmas party—a wonderland of sorts—was the perfect setting to let Violet know he'd like to spend time with her outside of their floral arrangement.

They finished giving the gifts, and Sean disappeared again. He couldn't wait for the party to die down, so he could take Violet some place special.

Once he shredded the Santa suit, Sean returned to the party, hoping to grab a dance with Violet before the night ended.

Unable to find her, Sean came up with an idea that he hoped showed Violet that he cared.

A short while later, Sean joined Jeff at his table with the cookie he decorated and the card he made.

"How's the evening treating you?" Jeff slapped Sean on the back.

Before Sean could answer, his gaze locked on Violet, and he wished he could erase the sight in front of him.

Sean's jaw clenched, his eyes burning with a fury so hot it threatened to consume him, fueled by the sight of Violet and the betrayal he felt.

Forgetting all about his conversation with Jeff, Sean's chest tightened. The older man's deep laugh burned Sean's insides like an itchy irritation.

"I see how your night is going."

Jealousy pounded in his gut. Seriously? Sean wouldn't allow himself . . .

His mind raced, desperate for answers, his heart pounding against his ribs as panic swelled. Why would Violet be dancing with Bruce McKay? He's a dirtbag.

Not that Sean thought he was the greatest man on earth, but he at least had respect for women.

Turning his attention back to Jeff, he asked, "If something happened to you, would you be upset with Katy if she started keeping company with another man?"

Keep company? Sean was talking like a man decades older than himself.

A serious expression replaced the former jovial look on Jeff's face. "I'll be with my Savior; nothing could upset me."

The change in music from *Silver Bells* to *I'll be Home for Christmas* gave Sean a glimmer of hope that Violet would seek him out. But she and McKay were still dancing.

Jeff never gave straight answers, and now didn't seem to be any different. However, if Sean didn't get answers soon, he might crack a tooth with how hard he was clenching his jaw.

"So if Katy died, you'd date again?"

Jeff rubbed his hand down his face. "Not being in that situation, I can't say yes or no for sure and would never judge anyone for the decisions they make." His face was tight, making Sean believe Jeff was holding out on him.

"By the way you're looking at Violet, I'd say you are in love with that woman."

Sean scoffed. "Love? Definitely not. We listen to each other. Violet makes sure that Sara's grave looks beautiful. She gives me space when I don't feel like talking. Sometimes all I wanted to do was sit and watch her make Sara's bouquets, and Violet doesn't pressure me at all."

"I hate to break it to you, Sean, my man, but that sounds an awful lot like love to me. The question is: what are you going to do about it?" Jeff paused when Katy showed up, dropping a kiss on his cheek.

"Who's in love?"

Jeff said, "Sean," at the same time Sean said, "No one."

She patted her husband on the chest. "That's old news, honey. Try to keep up." As she walked away, she winked at Sean.

"Every person is different, Sean. But I like to think I wouldn't be so closed off that if God handed me a stunning gift," he nodded his head toward Violet, "I would unwrap it and enjoy it for as long as God shared the gift with me."

Jeff leaned closer, throwing his thumb over his shoulder. "I sure as heck wouldn't let McKay anywhere near my woman."

Ouch! Jeff always knew what to say. Guilt ransacked Sean's chest. He'd overlooked Violet, but that was going to change. Right. Now.

Chapter 13

Bruce McKay blew in like a strong, unwelcomed air current the moment Sean left to change out of his Santa suit. How convenient.

He was one of the most narrow-minded men in Haven Ridge. Scratch that. He was the worst person in all of Montana.

"Darlin' loosen up," he guffawed, trying to pull her closer despite her resistance.

"Sorry, Bruce. I am not much of a dancer," she lied, wishing he would take that as a hint and leave her alone. She'd already ruined one of her favorite Christmas songs. She wouldn't be able to listen to *Silver Bells* for a long time.

Sadly, he wasn't good at reading the room. Bruce pulled her closer, stealing the breath from her lungs, destroying another Christmas classic for her.

Why hadn't Sean intervened? Their eyes had connected, but he kept talking to Jeff. *Did Sean think I wanted to dance with this clumsy oaf?*

Sean could take her breath away in the most magical way and dancing with him to *I'll Be Home For Christmas* seemed fitting since it might all be in her dreams, but oh what a dream it would be!

Desperation sat heavy on her chest. Violet's eyes darted around the room, hoping to find Sean so he could rescue her from this dance and send Bruce on his way, but he wasn't sitting with Jeff any longer.

A familiar sound rumbled behind her. "May I cut in?" Though Sean's voice remained steady, Violet couldn't miss the fiery emotion in his eyes, the clenched fist, and the set of his jaw.

Joy bloomed in her chest. Sean was there to rescue her. She'd analyze what it meant later. For now, she just wanted to be rid of Bruce Mckay.

Before she could respond, Bruce spoke up. "Sorry, Man. I waited all night. You snooze, you lose."

His gaze never left Violet's. "I'm asking you," Sean said, ignoring Bruce completely.

"I'd love that," Violet said, trying to push away from Bruce.

"Not going to happen, Lawrence."

Bruce twirled, or more like dragged Violet away from Sean, and the music came to a halt, grabbing everyone's attention.

"Look, there are a lot of kids here; don't make a scene," Violet pleaded with Bruce.

"What does he have that I don't have?"

Violet didn't want to upset the man since he was already squeezing her tighter than she was comfortable with, but she wouldn't lie, either.

"He's humble, kind, thoughtful, gentle."

"Gentle!" Bruce taunted.

Sean clasped his hand on Bruce's shoulder. "I suggest you let go of her, or you'll find out how *gentle* I am."

"Everything okay here?" Raddix and Damon asked as they approached behind Sean.

If Bruce would just let her go, there wouldn't be a scene, but Bruce was a first-class jerk and continued to prove it. It'd been at least a year since Violet had seen him at any of these events. She wondered what brought him here tonight, but Violet wouldn't ask and prolong this misery.

"We're fine, Son. You and Damon should go find out what Selena's doing here." He tilted his head toward the door.

Violet let out a sigh. "This night keeps getting worse. Bruce, please let me go. I'm not interested in dancing with you, talking to you—"

"I'm sure we could find something you'd like to do with me."

"Absolutely not!" She stated, appalled he'd make that insinuation.

She'd barely got the words out before Sean forced the man away from Violet. His fingers remained clutched on Bruce's shoulder. There was no mistake that Sean had found the man's pressure point and was using it to the fullest as he led Bruce outside.

Lily, Harlyn, and Katy were at Violet's side without delay. "Are you okay?" they asked in unison.

"Yeah, thanks to Sean." Violet let out a monstrous sigh, her lungs feeling free to breathe again.

"Let's go find out why Selena showed her face here," Harlyn suggested.

Ever since Damon kicked Selena off the ranch, she hadn't returned. Now, she dared enter the room with a cowboy on her arm and the ladies wanted to know her motive.

Closer to the door, Violet heard Sean letting Bruce know in no uncertain terms that he must stay away from her.

"What are you doing here, Selena?" Damon barked, and Harlyn placed her hand on his forearm, trying to help him remain calm.

The vicious blonde opened her mouth to speak, but closed it when Amelia spoke for her.

"I invited her," Amelia stepped in between Selena and Damon.

Uneasiness assaulted Violet. She'd heard about Selena's antics. No, it was more than antics. She was downright awful. Bullying Amelia throughout high school. Simultaneously using Raddix. As of late, Selena had tried to seduce Quinton, hoping he wouldn't fall for Amelia. She tried to rundown Raddix and Lily, coupled with her reckless threats to expose Harlyn to dangerous people from her past. That pushed Damon, a typically calm man, over the edge. He banished her from the ranch, making it clear she was never to return.

Until today, Amelia had supported Damon's actions.

"What gives Amelia?" Raddix asked, tense as ever.

Amelia stepped toward the men and their respective women and whispered, "Selena's dad is dying. He'll be lucky to make it to the new year."

The men's features softened. Probably because people liked Selena's dad, despite her actions.

"I promised him I would help her keep their ranch going. She's totally lost when it comes to anything on that ranch."

"Tell us something we don't know," Damon quipped.

Amelia gave Damon a *come on, give me a break* type look. "The man with her is Blake Johnson. I've hired him. He comes highly recommended as one of the best ranchers from Texas where Quinton used to work."

"After everything that barracuda has done to all of us, you're going to give her a free ride for the rest of her life?" Raddix didn't keep the disdain out of his tone.

Amelia shrugged. "Just because she's nasty doesn't mean I have to be. Mr. Whittaker is nervous about his daughter's future. I'm not giving her a free ride. She came onto Blake like she does every breathing man in Haven Ridge. I'm paying him to teach her how to operate the ranch. She will learn what it takes to keep her dad's ranch going when he's gone."

"I'm sure he loves his new job," Raddix chortled out a laugh.

"I had to throw in a weekly bonus for him to endure her innuendos. He's being as tolerant as one could expect."

"So we have to deal with her now?" Damon asked, crossing his arms.

"Not necessarily. She knows Blake works here and asked me if she could attend with her boyfriend if she promised to be on her best behavior."

"Boyfriend?" Raddix and Damon yelled together, shaking their heads.

"What are we missing? Does he only have a short time to live as well?" Lily tugged on Raddix's arm.

With her usual positivity and awareness of human nature, Lily allowed the psychologist within her to take control. "Honey, just because Selena isn't your favorite person doesn't mean someone can't love her. She could change."

Raddix kissed his wife on the temple. "I love you, Babe, but you're wrong this time."

"I'm proud of you for offering that olive branch, Dear," Violet addressed Amelia just as Selena and Blake approached the group.

The new *couple* stopped next to Amelia. "Thank you, Amelia, for letting me come," Selena began and then addressed the rest of the group. "I am very sorry for my past actions."

Silence reigned until Lily spoke. "Please don't expect us to trust you right away. We appreciate your apology, but your actions have negated your acknowledgement of wrongdoing before, so until we see a genuine change in you, we'll keep our distance."

"I understand." Selena's face twisted when she spoke, like it hurt to say those two simple words.

Violet didn't like fake people. Nor did she like to judge them, but Selena had made her own bed and that girl didn't look like she would change anytime soon.

Now that things were as settled as they could be, Sean leaned in and whispered in Violet's ear, "Can we have that dance now?"

Chapter 14

Sean led Violet to the dance floor where Hazel, Doris, and Myrtle were shuffling people all around, almost like they were clearing the floor for them. This put Sean on alert. These women were up to something.

Out of the corner of his eye, he watched Damon approach his daughter, who was face to face with Emmanuel. He wrapped his arm around her pre-teen waist and hoisted her away, leaving Emmanuel standing there alone.

"Put me down, Dad," Darlene screeched.

"You're too young to be kissing boys, no matter how great he is."

Emmanuel's fingers fiddled with the hem of his shirt, eyes darting around looking for. . . Amelia approached him and led him off to the side.

"Poor guy," Sean sympathized. "Rejection is hard at any age."

An older song that Hazel likely chose began playing. He appreciated the slowness of the music, but it'd taken forever and a day for the lyrics.

"Did you think I was going to reject you?" Sincerity oozed from Violet's lips.

Sean nodded, a lump in his throat preventing him from answering.

"Never."

That one simple word had his heart soared with excitement. Then the first two lines confirmed what he'd known all along.

I'd like you for Christmas

Please make my wish come true

As he gazed at her, something morphed in his chest, knowing that he forever needed this beautiful woman in his arms.

"Why were you dancing with Bruce?" He asked, not wanting this to drag on all night.

Violet's eyes widened, and she let out an audible sigh. "He wouldn't take no for an answer. When I agreed, thinking it would be one dance and over and done with, Bruce had other ideas, as you saw."

Sean wrapped both his arms around her waist, pulling her soft curves against his hard muscles. "I am sorry I didn't get here sooner. I hadn't seen you, so I decorated you a cookie and made you a card before I sat with Jeff. That's when I noticed you dancing."

"You did those things for me?" she asked, her voice warm and breathy.

"Yeah."

Her eyes lit up when she replied, "I can't wait to see them."

Sean felt his own smile grow when Violet rested her head on his chest, eliminating the space between them.

"Why didn't you rescue me sooner?" she asked, her voice soft and light.

Shoot! She saw him. *Tell her the truth.*

He kissed the top of her head. "I was angry and scared."

"Oh."

Beads of cold sweat pricked his skin, but the fire in his gut heated him throughout. Sean's fingers, clinging to her, needing comfort and reassurance, "I thought I was losing you."

"Sean," she began in a low, sweet voice that he felt in his chest. "Four years ago, I thought my life was over. I'd never had children, so when Marcus died, I was alone. It wasn't until I gave into Myrtle's pressure that I rejoined the land of the living and opened my flower shop."

His throat tightened. So he hoped she didn't expect him to speak anytime soon. Violet's words sparked a hot emotion behind his eyes. He hadn't cried since Sara's funeral.

Sean kissed the top of her head, encouraging Violet to continue with her feelings as Elvis's *Blue Christmas* came through the speakers.

Violet looked up into his eyes, and her intoxicating scent wafted through the crackling air between them, settling in his gut.

They shared a smile and his attraction to Violet saturated his heart with the sparkling tinsel and wreath decorations that came from this beautiful woman.

"I get it if you're not ready to move on—"

"Violet," Sean interrupted her, but she continued with her spiel.

"Losing someone, especially the way you did, is horrific. I thought we were getting close, but then you pulled away. I'm still not sure if that had to do with me or you. If you want to move on, but not with me, that, well, it sounds horrible, but I'll have to be fine with it if that's what you want because I care about you Sean Lawrence and if that means having to let you go then so be it."

Violet let out a sigh to end all sighs and he bit back a smile.

"Are you laughing at me?" Violet's feet froze, and she crossed her arms.

He wanted to take her out of her misery, so he leaned down and brushed a soft kiss on her unsuspecting lips.

When he pulled back, her fingers brushed her bottom lip. "What was that for?"

Sean looked up, pointing at a sprig of mistletoe, and a bubble of laughter escaped from both of them. "Besides, I want to tell you something, and that was the only way to get you to stop talking."

"That's the best way anyone has ever gotten me to be quiet," she said, sharing a laugh with him.

He pulled her flush with him again and picked up their dance once again. "First, I am sorry for getting flowers from Randall. I've been confused and didn't know how to handle it, so I did what I do best and isolated myself."

She opened her mouth, maybe to apologize, but he cut her off quickly, not wanting her to do so for something that wasn't her fault.

"I don't want to move on. . ."

Violet's disappointed eyes dropped, but he lifted her chin with his finger and finished.

". . .with anyone but you."

Her cheeks flushed pink with excitement, her eyes sparkling with delight, a grin splitting her face.

"My heart yearns to give you the best, but I cannot promise perfection; life is messy. I am the most imperfect man you'll ever meet." They continued to sway to Elvis's Christmas classic. "I'm scared," he admitted for her ears only.

"You are safe with me, Sean Lawrence—you and your heart."

His heart stalled when her words registered in his mind. Then it beat out of rhythm, making him winded.

Sean gently pulled her hand away from his biceps and kissed her palm. "Thank you. I hunger for the connection that has come from being with you," his voice, low and vulnerable.

"Sara and Marcus will always be a part of us, and I'll never ask you to forget her or put me above her. I know my heart has plenty of room for you and Marcus, so I'm hoping your heart has room for me, too."

"I've got a suite with your name on it," he hung his head. "That was really cheesy, wasn't it?"

She bit her smiling lip and nodded. "But it was super sweet and I appreciate the sentiment."

Violet laced her fingers with his and rested them against Sean's chest to finish out the dance.

Thank you, Lord, for your will and the courage to get my girl.

"Here's to the next stage of our life. Together." Sean wrapped his arms around Violet's waist and pulled her off the floor as she released a cute squeal.

"You are my future. Thank you for being patient with me," he said before he kissed her soft lips with a tenderness that hopefully told her she was safe with him, too.

Everyone rushed to them, surrounding them on the dance floor. Raddix hugged his dad, and Myrtle hugged Violet.

"The girls and I knew you were meant for each other, so we didn't have to do anything to push you together. That means we can save our ideas for the next couple in Haven Ridge."

It was impossible not to fall for this woman. He was incredibly grateful for Violet's patience and vowed to make her happy.

Chapter 15

Christmas Eve day left Violet exhausted. She'd sold over one hundred arrangements this week, and couldn't wait to relax at the ranch with Sean and the group she considered family.

She reached the barn door, and just as she was about to push it open, a cow let out a deep, resonant moo, spoiling her attempt at a surprise.

"Violet? You got here quickly."

They'd both been nonstop since the party, only making time to see each other when they watched Tanner win Nationals.

Not that they didn't want to spend time together, but it was only in movies and books where couples didn't seem to work once they got together.

Real life was different. Work didn't disappear. Sean and Violet would figure a schedule that made sense for them.

Meeting in the barn would be something they did regularly for the next three months, as Sean had a barn full of heifers scheduled to give birth between January and March.

"Tanner just arrived and everyone's ready to start the party, so I offered to come get you."

Sean washed and dried his hands before he attempted to hug her, which she appreciated.

"Let me look at you," Sean beamed, gripping her waist. "You are a sight."

"Please. I'm in a pair of jeans and a sweater. You act like I'm Naomi Campbell or Cindy Crawford."

"Have you seen yourself in those jeans?"

Violet laughed, but underneath, elation filled her soul when Sean compared her to a supermodel. As if.

He pressed his lips to hers, letting them dance together with enough passion to power the electric fence surrounding the cattle.

Violet slid her hands up Sean's chest and around his neck, weaving her fingers through the hair at Sean's nape.

The low rumble from his throat sent a current down her spine, filling her with a wave of pure joy that lapped over Violet.

A long while later, they pulled away from each other, breathless. Sean dropped his forehead to hers and rubbed his hands up and down her arms.

"Are you ready to go in?" she asked, unsure if she was ready for that herself.

Spending time alone with Sean, kissing for hours, seemed like the perfect plan, but the kids' boundless Christmas Eve excitement made that impossible.

"I'd like to show you something before we go in, if you don't mind."

Sean left the barn, holding the door for Violet. He sidled up to her after securing the door, brushing their shoulders against each other with every stride.

"Where are you taking me?"

Sean wrapped his arms around her. "You'll see."

The kids helped decorate the split-rail fences around the property with garland adorn in half moons, making the ranch sparkle in the winter sunshine or moonlight depending on the time of day.

Violet had never ventured beyond the barn for the Christmas party, so seeing all this was a big deal. Her eyes darted from the expansive apple orchard to the extra large greenhouses that housed more crops than Violet had ever seen.

"These cabins are for the ranch hands."

"Is yours close by?" Violet asked, tucking her chin when Sean gave her questioning eyes.

"Ms. Skillings, are you propositioning me?"

Adrenaline surged through her veins, fueled by sheer panic. "No. I didn't mean anything by it. I mean, you know where I live, so I was just—"

Sean interrupted her with a burst of laughter. "I'm just teasing you."

They continued walking—four rows of cabins later, Sean offered, "That one on the end is mine."

A flurry of butterflies danced in her stomach, their wings a whirlwind of excitement, making her heart beat faster. Sean shared where he lived with her; leaving her speechless.

Sean offered the explanation, "Storage barns," as Violet's jaw dropped in surprise at the sight of six large barns, tucked away and unknown to most people. Seeing the rest of the ranch with fresh eyes gave her a thrilling sense of discovery and love. If Sean didn't trust her, he wouldn't show her this area, right?

A few moments later, the sound of rushing water caught Violet's attention. "Please tell me you're not taking me in that." She pointed at the river they were approaching.

"Are you afraid of water?" Sean chuckled, tugging her toward the current.

She shook her head. "Not when it's ninety degrees out, but when it's twenty, and we have almost a foot of snow, I frown against swimming outdoors."

"Where's your adventure?"

"Staying warm."

He stopped her in front of a small cemetery. A massive headstone bore the name Lawrence. Two-foot stones laid about a foot in front of the large name plot. One read Jack and the other read Marilyn—Amelia's parents.

Another foot stone about two feet to the right of Marilyn's read Sara. Next to Sara's was the small wreath she'd made and given to Sean.

Emotion overwhelmed Violet. Sean brought her to Sara's gravesite. This was huge.

Then he surprised her even more by lacing their fingers together. "Sara, this is Violet. I know you know her, but she's the woman I've been talking about. Thank you for giving me your blessing. She's a strong woman who can keep me in line."

Violet smiled at the thought of her keeping Sean in line. It was beyond her wildest dreams that she could ever do something like that.

"I haven't been doing so great since you left me, but now that I've let Violet in, I can feel it—I'm a better man because of her. I have purpose again."

"Hi, Sara. Sean is just being modest. I'm sure you're used to that. He loves you so much. I hope to be half the woman you were. I'll do everything I can to take care of him."

Sean squeezed her shoulder as he guided her back to the house. "You know it's not a competition, right?"

"Yeah, I wasn't implying that it would be. You're a great man, so she must have been remarkable—"

Sean stopped her on the path. "Wait a second," he interrupted. "You are an amazing woman yourself." He paused and swallowed hard, like he wanted to say more, but wasn't sure how.

An electricity in the air crackled around them. He leaned closer. Instead of capturing her lips, his stubble gently scraped her cheek, and the world faded around her the more he filled her space. "Violet," his warm breath, hot on her cheek, sent shivers down her spine. He whispered, "I love you."

Violet swallowed hard, trying to process Sean's words. "You love me? For real?" She pressed her hand to her chest.

"Yes," he chortled out a breath. "Why are you so shocked? You're a beautiful, smart, creative, kind, patient woman."

A wave of emotion washed over her, bringing tears to the brim of her eyes. Her heart had belonged to him for a long time, but he was the one who finally spoke the words she'd longed to hear.

"Sean. I love you, too!" She caressed his forearms. His corded muscles flexed under her fingers, and she pulled him in for a sweet kiss.

Everything about that gentle kiss helped Violet realize Sean was her future. It wouldn't be easy, but nothing important ever was.

There was no turning back now—both she and Sean were fully invested in their future together.

Thank you for reading Sean and Violet's love story. The sheriff and Willow are next. Keep reading and you'll find chapter 1 of The Perfect Sheriff for your enjoyment. Please note: it is unedited at this point, so I apologize for any grammar or typo you may come across. I'm banking on you being too intrigued to notice!

How About a Review?

Your feedback is valuable, so please consider sharing your thoughts. This will help other readers discover this book and my other works.

Thank you from the bottom of my heart for reading and reviewing my book(s).

Amazon

Goodreads

Bookbub

Chapter 1 – The Perfect Sheriff

I t was mid winter, the make-it-through-the-cold-season... Have you ever considered the notion that you are just a meticulously groomed cattle? Gerard had... The auctioneers, three troublesome, but loving septuagenarians, had been calling his number... Initially subtle — a low thrumming, like a distant drumbeat of doom, rumbling in his chest, growing steadily stronger until he could hear the barter holler vibrating through his very bones. The time to protest was now ... Sweat, thick as air, ran down Gerard's back as he inhaled. Letting that breath out slowly, he locked eyes on his target and stepped into the diner...

Gerard cleared his throat as he approached the back of the diner. Myrtle, Hazel, and Doris huddled over papers scattered on the table, too preoccupied to even notice him. No doubt orchestrating their next scheme, hence his unease.

Be sure to leave me out of your shenanigans.

"Morning, ladies."

"Sheriff." Doris looked up from the scribbles she wrote on one sheet.

"You know, Eisenhower used less paper planning D-Day. Please tell me that whatever you are conjuring up won't land you in my jail cell."

He startled, his eyes widening. Possibly because of Myrtle's hooting laughter or her hot pink leggings and black shirt with neon green flames that burned his retina. Either way, the place reeked of gossip and mischievousness, telling him to leave immediately before he gave them any fuel for their fragile hope that he would fall madly in love and keep their matchmaking record secure.

Myrtle was still laughing. She even threw in a few knee slaps, most likely to prevent him from asking more questions. No such luck. He had more patience for the ladies than anyone else in town even after what they did to him after the festival a few months back.

"Seriously, what plan are you hatching up?" When the women, perfectly coined The Troublesome Trio, hadn't responded, Gerard continued. "I'd prefer not to be involved in your plans. I think two hours in a shed with the pastor's daughter was enough meddling for a lifetime."

Who trapped people against their will anyway? Apparently, these ladies. Other couples in Haven Ridge had shared their stories of matchmaking and were happily connected with their soul mate. But not him. He was fine as the single sheriff. The last thing he wanted was another relationship to blow up in his face.

Full disclosure, he hadn't complained about being trapped in the shed either. If he was being honest, during that time with Willow, he saw her inner strength and alluring charm shine through. Her hazel eyes, filled with desperation, had finally softened and begged him to rescue her, and he had, in a way. He was the one to call his deputy and tell him to rush to the church and free them before his phone died.

He swallowed a lump in his throat when he recalled how her silky blonde hair cascaded down his arm when she leapt onto his lap at the sight of a scurrying mouse. Willow refused to leave his lap until the door opened. He felt a profound gratitude for the small creature.

For those two hours, her coldness toward him had almost vanished. He couldn't remember the last time a simple touch breathed life into him, an foreign awareness he rather enjoyed.

Yet, lingering issues remained.

Willow was the pastor's daughter, and he was intimidating, especially to a man with Gerard's past, but he wasn't ready to let everyone know about that. Furthermore, he continued to question his and Willow's age difference, past kissing debacle, and her seven year absence. Though all of these were reasonable concerns, it didn't explain why Willow gave him attitude.

He shouldn't have been surprised though. No woman had ever considered him good enough to stick around, including his mom. Who could blame them? His less-than-honorable past caused him to keep his distance. Willow deserved a good man.

What was he? He'd say a five out of ten, if anyone asked for his opinion, but that was not good enough. Not for Willow.

"We apologized for that," Hazel interrupted his thoughts before he trudged any further down the pity path he'd traveled many times before.

"The wind blew the door shut," Myrtle's tone, less than convincing.

"Okaaay," he said, disbelieving.

If he was to believe any one of the three women, it would be Hazel Evans. She was more of a mother to him when he first arrived than his own had ever been. Despite being full of energy, she was more calm and quiet than the other two. That is probably due to owning the diner with her husband. She'd never scare customers away, on purpose.

Doris Barnes, the second most dangerous with information, sat directly across from Hazel. Doris's eyes were as mischievous as her smile. However, if you got her mad, watch out! Gerard recalled the perfectly primped woman in front of him standing on a chair telling an unwanted visitor how things were going to go.

Then, there was Myrtle Hill. She was the ringleader when it came to schemes. She never hid her stunts. He knew from experience. A vivid memory of this woman blasted through his mind. She'd hit that same unwanted visitor with her purse before one of the cowboys could stop her.

"It really was a misunderstanding, Sheriff," Hazel cooed.

Okay. Now his trust in Hazel had diminished a fraction.

"Yet, one of you put a bar between the handles, trapping us in there for hours until Jimmy rescued us."

"Sorry, Sheriff, but our crew is here," Myrtle pointed toward the door as they gathered their papers and shuffled off.

Of all the... Gerard silently exclaimed. He never got straight answers from these women. No one did.

A bell rang at the open window between the diner and the kitchen. Frank, Hazel's husband, spotted Gerard. "Morning, Sheriff. I think you're next."

Gerard looked between Frank and the trio. His face must have reflected pure fright, causing the owner to laugh. Before he escaped into the thralls of his kitchen he said, "Don't fight it. You'll lose."

Would it be so bad to lose? Willow was so easy to talk to when she wasn't sassing him. That sneaky thought gave him a sudden urge to spill his guts. Would she care to listen? Even thinking about growing closer to her seemed ludicrous. He needed to get his mind focused back on the action happening in his town.

He smiled at the entourage of community members pouring. Best town ever, no doubt about that. Being the sheriff here was an honor. These people were his family. A pang of despair shot through Gerard's chest when he watched a few of the married couples doting on each other. Would he ever find a beautiful woman to be with? *Lord, please. You gave Adam one, saying that man needed a companion. I'd appreciate one that won't tempt me to commit condemning sins, though, thanks.*

"Hello, everyone! Rohan is here!" The owner of the dance hall entered like he was announcing himself as the next contestant on a gameshow.

Gerard made a face. Oh, brother. This could get interesting.

"Who's ready to plan the Valentine's Day dance?" he asked in his boisterous voice, often used when acting as the DJ during events.

Not him. Gerard pulled out his phone, checking the time, wondering how he'd get out of the diner without insulting anyone.

Ah ha. An idea came to him. "Where's Randall this morning? Doesn't he usually join the group?" Gerard asked.

"Not always. Sometimes he can't find anyone to man the store," Violet, the flowershop owner shared.

"I hear congratulations are in order," Gerard heard Cora say to Violet.

"Thank you," Violet gushed, holding up her left hand, eyes sparkling. "Sean gave it to me on Christmas. We won't walk down the aisle anytime soon, but he said he wanted everyone to know that I was his."

Cora's lips curved up in a smile. "That's wonderful. Baby steps are better than nothing." Her eyes darted to Gerard.

Good grief. A bead of cold sweat popped out on his forehead, slick and cold against his skin. *Was Willow's mom implying that I should make a plea for her daughter? Does she know something I don't?*

With a nervous gulp, Gerard clutched his coffee mug as if it were a lifeline, his eyes darting around the room, desperately trying to avoid Cora's piercing stare. Uneasiness gnawed at him. Could Willow's parents ever embrace him if they knew about his past?

"Sheriff, are you going to join us?" Cora's pleasant voice silenced the room as she gestured to the chair next to hers.

Gerard, avoider of dating and socializing, let the question linger in the air, causing him to tense as all eyes fixed on him.

Despite being over a foot shorter and at least a hundred pounds lighter, Willow's mom had an intimidating power over him, just like her husband. They were good people and he was a former criminal. What more did he have to say?

Carrying that weight around all these years was taxing. More than that, he'd worked hard to hide the growing feelings blossoming in his chest for Willow.

Besides the Troublesome Trio and Lily, who caught Gerard ogling Willow at the summer festival, nobody knew he was interested in the pastor's daughter. Heck, he only admitted it to himself a week ago. Thinking about Willow's sweet mother potentially turning rabid if she found out a former criminal wanted more than friendship with her daughter made him cringe.

If he was lucky, maybe Willow would join them today? Whenever she didn't have a client, Willow was an active participant in town activities. Maybe he should wait a little longer to see if she arrived?

"Willow usually sits here, but she's running errands and can't join us today."

That answered that.

He shook his head. "I wish I could, but I'm going on patrol. Randall's store is my first stop." He should be here. After losing his wife a couple of years ago, he'd drowned himself in work. Getting together with the other business owners in town was his only social interaction, besides his customers.

One could accuse him of drowning himself in work, too, but he had no choice, right? He had a whole town to protect.

Meanwhile, he found himself enjoying bantering with the fiery hairdresser and had made a New Year's resolution to stop isolating himself, at least when it came to her. How pathetic was he? Very. She would stomp all over his heart and he'd be picking up the pieces before Valentine's Day. Yet, he couldn't stop himself from gravitating toward her.

James and his dad, Harvey from the hardware store, which also served as the feed store for the ranchers, entered last and found a place at the table. Studying the menu, Harvey said, "We have to scarf down our food and run. We don't feel comfortable leaving the store unattended for too long."

"No offense, Sheriff," James quickly filled in for his dad.

He knew they were referring to the string of unsolved break-ins, the ones that had his entire town on edge. A wave of guilt washed over Gerard, heavy and suffocating, each pang a painful reminder of the criminal still running free.

Between him and his deputy, they were patrolling their entire shift, leaving the station void of any authority. Only the town's dispatcher could be found at the station. Gerard made sure the doors were locked, but that wouldn't stop a determined criminal.

This wasn't the way he'd wanted to start his morning. First Cora, then Harvey. Gerard felt the urge to remove his hat and wipe the sweat from his brow, but that seemed too revealing, given that it was the first week of January and only twenty-two degrees out.

"Hopefully, sometime soon, you can—"

A loud screech blared through his police radio, cutting Violet's words short.

"Dispatch to Sheriff."

He pressed the button on the side of the device, resting on his shoulder. "Go ahead, dispatch."

"Robbery in progress at Randall Brown's store. The offender has fled on foot. Age approximately sixteen, a yellow hoodie, jeans—two sizes too big—and bright white sneakers. He is said to be armed and potentially dangerous."

Gerard set down his mug and was at the door as a chorus of *"be safe; get 'em, Sheriff; put on your vest; let us know,"* reached his ears. He lifted a hand to acknowledge their well-wishes, pushed open the door, and let dispatch know he was en route.

Acknowledgements

"And whatever you do, in word or deed, do everything in the name of the Lord Jesus, giving thanks to God the Father through him." —Colossians 3:17

Writing and sharing my stories with the world is a privilege. This is an enormous responsibility, and I couldn't do it without support.

My dear readers, your support means the world to me. I cherish every one of you. It means a lot to me that you spent time with Sean, Violet, and the Haven Ridge gang, even though you could be reading any number of captivating Christmas stories right now.

Laura, thank you for your unwavering commitment to maintaining continuity, not just in this book, but throughout the series. You reminded me that my characters' faith is a central theme in my story, and their prayers needed to be heard.

To my amazing ARC readers, thanks for sharing the love and spreading the word about my book. I appreciate your support! Your effort in reading, providing insightful reviews, and sharing your comments is incredibly valuable.

Lissa, your supportive nature shines through in your creative collages, which you always make sure to share. Amazing! I am honored to have met you!

Linda, you've been a constant source of support and guidance, always ready to teach me the ins and outs of this community. You taught me how to make a cover! It's hard to fathom that it's been nearly three years since that happened! You are the best author friend I could ever ask for; thank you!

Finally, I want to express my heartfelt appreciation to my family, who not only support my writing but also create lasting memories with me which help nurture my creativity and ignite my enthusiasm for each new tale.

About the Author

Karen Tucci, a public school teacher by profession, now tutors writing students online and homeschools her two children.

A native of Maine, she has trekked miles of the Pine Tree State and visited countless others. It is through her life experiences that the basis for her romance stories develop. One of her favorite things to say when out adventuring is, "...that is definitely going in my next book!"

Fun fact: Karen had only read and wrote non-fiction growing up. It wasn't until her late twenties that she embraced the joy brought forth by doing both — reading and writing — within the different romance tropes. Now she reads at least fifteen fiction novels a month and writes daily!

Connect with Karen:

Facebook Reader's Group.

To find out about special deals, giveaways, and new releases, join her newsletter:

https://www.trueheartromance.com

Instagram

Goodreads

Bookbub

Amazon